CAROL LIU

WITH MARYBETH SIDOTI CALDARONE

ARLENE, THE REBEL QUEEN

EMERALD
BOOK CO.

Published by Emerald Book Company
Austin, TX
www.emeraldbookcompany.com

Distributed by Emerald Book Company
For ordering information or special discounts for bulk purchases, please contact Emerald Book Company at PO Box 91869, Austin, TX 78709, 512.891.6100.

Design, cover design, and composition by Greenleaf Book Group LLC
Cover illustration by Mark Minnig

Publisher's Cataloging-In-Publication Data
(Prepared by The Donohue Group, Inc.)

Liu, Carol.
  Arlene, the rebel queen / Carol Liu with Marybeth Sidoti Caldarone.—1st ed.
    p. ; cm.
  Summary: Inspired by a social studies unit on our country's biggest social movements, and perhaps prompted by the cafeteria's overflowing garbage cans, Arlene and her friends launch a campaign to reduce their school's carbon footprint. Like most rebellions, they face stiff opposition, in this case from principal Musgrove. While leading this revolution, Arlene finds herself marching farther away from the friend she always thought would be there.
  Interest age level: 006-012.
  ISBN: 978-1-937110-50-5

  1. Student movements—Juvenile fiction. 2. Environmental responsibility—Juvenile fiction. 3. Friendship—Juvenile fiction. 4. Children with disabilities—Juvenile fiction. 5. Environmental responsibility—Fiction. 6. Friendship—Fiction. 7. Physically handicapped–Fiction. I. Caldarone, Marybeth Sidoti. II. Title.
PZ7.L5832 As 2013
[Fic]   2012954726

Part of the Tree Neutral® program, which offsets the number of trees consumed in the production and printing of this book by taking proactive steps, such as planting trees in direct proportion to the number of trees used: www.treeneutral.com

Printed in the United States of America on acid-free paper

13 14 15 16 17 18   10 9 8 7 6 5 4 3 2 1

First Edition

*This book is dedicated to
all children growing up with CMT
—you have the power!*

CONTENTS

To the Dreamers

Dreams are dreamt.
Many are just spent.
Several are reaching for the bright, shining stars.
Some are asking for the bright rainbow to take them away,
Away from the pain they have to pay.
Some dreams are asking favors from the love-struck Cupid.
Not one dream is stupid.
Every dream dreamt has a special meaning in life.
Not one is impossible.

If you are able to dream it,
Then you surely can make it true.
Just have trust in your dreams.
Don't forget your dreams.
They are an important part of you!

By Marah Griffith, a young woman who wrote beautiful poetry to express her feelings about growing up with Charcot-Marie-Tooth disease.

FOREVER FRIEND?

My Uncle James says that change is like a wave crashing in at Scarborough Beach. If you're lucky, you see it coming. (Sometimes you don't, and it knocks your face into the salty surf.) If you do see it start to roar toward you, he says, you've basically got two choices: fight it or ride it. Fight it, and you can get slammed. Ride it, and you can have the time of your life. But you can also end up shipwrecked in some totally weird, totally uncomfortable place.

At the beginning of fifth grade, this idea kept popping into my head, with a big *ba-bing*! I was dealing with some pretty big changes that year.

Now, those of you who heard about me in fourth grade might be saying to yourselves, "What?! Didn't she have to deal with *leg braces* in fourth grade?"

Well, yes, okay, that was pretty humongous. But after those few shaky weeks in the fall, that year kind of smoothed out. Remember? The kids in my class got to know each other better, and eventually we were all singing in "har-mo-neee!" as my music teacher would say.

Fifth grade, on the other hand, was very rocky. I guess I felt the first rumble of the changes to come that one Friday in October. I made my way down the aisle of the bus—yes, in my leg braces. They're like soccer shin guards, except they cover the back of my leg, not the front. They help keep my ankles and knees steady while I walk. They're supposed to keep me from falling, but they weren't doing a very good job that year. Anyway, that terrible Friday, my troubles started. I found my seat on the bus, right next to my best friend, Lauren, just like always. It's a short ride to my stop, the first one. So I had to make plans with Lauren fast.

"So we'll pick you up at nine tomorrow, okay?" I said to Lauren as the bus lurched forward.

"Um . . . yeah . . . well . . . I think I may not go tomorrow, Arlene," Lauren said, staring out the window, fingering one of her dark brown curls.

"What? Why?" I leaned forward to see her face, but that was a mistake. The bus heaved itself around the corner, and without the extra support of the seat back, I crashed onto Lauren. "Oh, sorry!"

Lauren sighed. "It's okay," she said as she gently pushed me off her. "Arlene, I think I'm going to go ice skating tomorrow morning. . . with Maddie. We're going to start figure skating practice in a few weeks, with that team I joined, and I need to get ready."

Well, that was weird. Ice skating—obviously that didn't include me! "But you always go to the stable with me," I said. "I thought you liked brushing the horses."

Lauren had been going with me to my therapeutic horseback riding classes almost the whole summer. She would watch during my lesson as my teacher helped me ride a horse named Fox. Fox was so cool, all strong and muscular, but really gentle. I felt like the queen of the world on his back. The class lasted only a half hour, and afterward Lauren and I got to brush some of the horses, although we spent most of the time with Fox. We'd pet his big, soft nose, and feed him lots of carrots. Horseback riding supposedly improved my core strength. I didn't know what core strength was, I didn't know I had any to begin with, and I didn't really care about improving it. I just liked horses.

"But this is the only time this weekend that I

can go to open skate," Lauren said. "I really need to practice." She looked at me and seemed kind of worried. Maybe she was afraid I'd be mad, so I tried to lighten things up with a joke.

"Oh, sure, you just wanna hang out with the TABs this week. I know how you are." And I looked at her out of the corner of my half-closed eyes, with a half-smirk, so she'd know I was being sarcastic.

But somehow she must not have ever learned that all these half-things—like half a laugh, half a smile, half-closed eyes—usually mean someone's joking. As the bus cruised down the hill on the way to my street, things took a wrong turn for Lauren and me.

"What are you talking about?" Lauren twisted in her seat so she was completely facing me. "What in the world is a TAB? And this has nothing to do with choosing to hang out with anybody. This is about skating!"

"Okay, calm down. It was a *joke!*" I said, laughing to show her even more clearly what she should be doing right about now. "A TAB is a temporarily able-bodied person. My physical therapist told me that. Get it? A TAB! It's like, everyone is only temporarily *not* disabled. Someday, even you'll get all old and feeble." I bent over in my seat, put a hand on my back, squinted my eyes and puckered my mouth, all for the best demonstration of a wrinkled old lady that I could muster up.

Lauren didn't even laugh at my old lady impression. She just stared at me.

What was going on? I thought it was hilarious when I heard what TAB meant. It's kind of true and really funny all at the same time.

"That's just rude all the way around, Arlene," Lauren shouted over the squeal of the bus tires as we swerved onto my street. "I'm not a TAB! And I'm not old and feeble. And everything isn't always about you. Maybe I'm tired of watching you trot around in a circle all morning!"

Whoa! As I think about this conversation now, I can see where her feelings got hurt, and I should have chosen a much kinder thing to say. But see, my feelings got all fired up at this point too. And the bus was slowing down to my stop. So, yeah, I didn't help things much.

"Maybe you should lighten up! I'm just trying to talk to you, joke around, and you're *freaking out*."

Lauren whipped herself around and looked out the window again. So, of course, I kept talking, trying to get some kind of reaction. I hate it when people ignore me—it's my weak spot, really.

"Never mind," I shouted right back at her. "Don't come tomorrow. Don't come ever!"

She ignored me. Again.

The bus screeched to a stop near my house. I stood up and looked at Lauren and couldn't think of anything to say, anything to do. How did we get to this awful place?

I turned and worked myself and my backpack up the aisle. Lauren was my new "Bus Buddy," the person who was assigned to help me on and off the bus. Apparently people felt that my legs had gotten too weak to safely get me on and off the bus. Whatever.

I wasn't surprised that Lauren had clearly just quit her job. She didn't follow me up to the door like she was supposed to, and I didn't look back. I started stepping slowly off the bus, pushing against the door hard with my fist, all balled up like I was ready to punch someone—which I was.

Mrs. Kracken, our bus driver, lifted her face to the rearview mirror, which made the saggy skin under her chin stretch out like a rubber band. She called out with her thick Rhode Island accent, "Ah-lene! Wait! Wheah's yaw helpah?" Her gray hair fell out of its loose braid as she whipped her head around to search the aisle. "Hey!" she shouted again. "Wheah's Ah-lene's helpah?"

She might have just as well screamed into a megaphone that a poor, sick, helpless, pathetic baby was about to plunge to her death unless some angel named Lauren swooped in to save her.

I could make it down these steps myself. I certainly didn't need *her* to help me. The last step was tricky, but I bent down very low, almost sitting on the bottom step, and eased myself onto the street. Humph! Helper, help-ah, whatever you wanted to call it, I didn't need one!

I shuffled up my driveway, grinding street sand beneath my high top sneakers, enjoying the gritty sound. Lauren and I had had arguments before, but this one felt deeper. What would I do if I didn't have her as my forever friend?

CALM BEFORE THE STORM

Uncle James would know about change. His life had changed in a big way on September 2. His wife, who is my mom's sister, had a baby on that day. So of course we had to go see the baby.

After my huge fight with Lauren on Friday and my lonely horseback-riding lesson on Saturday, we got up early Sunday to head to New York City. Traveling to see Aunt Marie and Uncle James is always stressful because New York is not like Rhode Island. For some reason, there's nowhere to park in the city except in expensive garages that Dad doesn't like to pay for. So, we ride around and around, looking for a space, only to end up in a garage an hour later because Dad is a terrible parallel parker and he can never make our big van fit into the street spaces.

Then there's Uncle James's apartment, which has four steps up to the front door. That means Mom has to take her manual wheelchair, which either Dad or my older brother Chris has to push and bump up the steps. Her motorized one (*don't* call it an electric wheelchair—Mom always says, "I'm not being executed!") is just too big to go up steps, and so without a ramp, she's trapped. But Mom really likes her big motorized chair better because she can *move* whenever she wants to. Otherwise she feels like a statue.

So when we got to the city, we paid all that money for a garage, shook Chris awake from the snorty nap he took the whole way there, bumped Mom up the stairs to the building, and finally made it to Uncle James's apartment. When you first go in, boom! You're in the living room right away. Then to the left, you think it's a closet, but no, that's the kitchen. Keep going forward about three steps, and there's one more room, the bedroom/office/storage room/and now, baby room. And that's about it. Oh, and a bathroom. But, of course, Mom can't fit in there, so we can only stay at Uncle James's house so long, even if we stop at a rest-stop bathroom right before we get there.

I heard Mom say something about how the new

baby will force Uncle James to finally move to a bigger apartment. That seems like a lot of power for one tiny little baby.

Mom and Aunt Marie squealed and kissed and oohed and ahhed. Little Zoe, celebrity-star-super-baby, was in Aunt Marie's arms and looked . . . well, like an ordinary baby to me. Not really very exciting. Chris plopped down on the couch, plugged himself into his music, and tuned the rest of us out. Nice.

I wanted to see Uncle James right away, so I walked into the back room and found him sitting at his tiny desk, typing at lightning speed. Uncle James and I are cool. We get each other.

"Hey, Uncle James!" I called.

Tip-tap-tip-tap-tap.

"Uncle James!" I tried again. (When he's typing, it usually takes two or three tries to stop him. I don't mind. Like I said, I get him.)

Uncle James pulled his eyes away from the computer, very slowly like his forehead was attached by thick rubber bands to the screen. Finally, his eyes reached me and focused. "Hey! What's happening? When did you get here?"

"Um, right now."

"Well, c'mere. Give me a hug, Curly-Whirley."

Uncle James walked around to the front of the

desk and gave me a big squeeze. He always calls me the goofiest names. It's our thing.

I hugged my uncle right back. You see, he's a little different, just like me. Uncle James is my only Chinese uncle. And as I learned last year during that crazy school election, differences are definitely something to be celebrated.

For example, Uncle James showed us this really cool Chinese thing called dim sum. At dim sum restaurants, the waiters push carts filled with little dishes of food around the room. You point at stuff that looks good, and they plop it on your table. There are only about two or three pieces of food on the little dishes, so you've got to keep pointing. The waiters keep plopping, and the carts keep rolling around. There are dumplings, sticky rice, spring rolls, and soft buns with meat inside. Everything's really yummy.

But I have to warn you, if you're going to try dim sum, you might see chicken feet—for real! Chicken. Feet. Uncle James loves them. I actually tried them. I just closed my eyes and bit off a toe, covered in this brown, gooey sauce. I spit out the bone like I saw Uncle James do, and chewed on the skin, which would have been tasty except I couldn't stop my imagination. What if I accidentally swallowed a toenail? Or what if the chicken stepped in chicken poop right before he got cooked and served in this restaurant? How could a one-footed chicken possibly cross the road?

Anyway, back to Uncle James. He isn't just different because he's Chinese. He also has a really different kind of job. He's "the people's lawyer," he says. He works for a group of civil rights lawyers, fighting for equal rights for all people. Apparently, not everyone has equal rights yet. I thought they did, but based on how hard Uncle James works, I'm guessing not.

So this is why we get each other. As a Chinese lawyer fighting for equal rights when most people think everyone already has them, Uncle James is different. And I'm different, living with Charcot-Marie-Tooth disease. I have to deal with wearing leg braces, a lot of falling (which has really been driving me crazy lately), and not being able to tie my shoes anymore (what am I, a kindergartener all over again?).

In case you don't know, Charcot-Marie-Tooth disease is something people are born with. It's basically a problem in your genes that makes your nerves just slowly stop working as you grow older. With messed-up nerves, your muscles don't hear your brain talking to them, so it gets harder and harder for you to move your feet, legs, fingers, and hands. My mom has CMT, too, but my dad and brother don't. It's a disease that gets passed down, but there's only a fifty percent chance you'll get it from your parent. And sometimes, it pops out of nowhere, like it did with Mom.

There are lots of different types of CMT. Sometimes you can't even tell a person has it, and other kinds, like with Mom and me, you can tell right away. Mom uses a wheelchair to get around, and she can't move her fingers at all anymore. Except for that index finger on her right hand, which she shakes at you when she's really mad. I've had that happen way too many times, especially last year when all that mess happened with the boy-girl war.

I can still walk but I have to use leg braces because my knees and ankles are really getting weak. My braces aren't bright purple like my first ones were, and they don't have floating butterflies on them. I am ten after all, and I figured I needed a more grown-up look. But not a boring one! So I put pink camouflage duct tape all over my grown-up, plain-white braces. They look much better now.

I still lose my balance a lot, even with my braces. My fingers are getting weaker too, although I can still write and pick up stuff. But spinning a spinner on a game is tough, and unfortunately, just as I'm about ready to talk my parents into getting me a cell phone, it's getting harder and harder to push buttons. What in the world is the point of a cell phone if I can't text?

Anyway, after we did our hug thing, Uncle James sat on the edge of his desk to face me head on. He crossed his arms and stared right into my eyes. "What's up this year at school? What's your plan?"

It's true, I was hoping to come with a new Big Plan, something to top last year as class president and being a pretty popular girl in the school. But then in July I got really busy at this cool sailing camp for kids who live with a disability, and in August I got busy with all the family that came to visit us (they love the beach!). I kind of just ran out of time.

"I'm thinking I might lie low this year. Just kind of hang out with my friends, focus on school, maybe relax."

Uncle James put both hands on the sides of his head, covering his ears, like those words stung his eardrums. Then he shook his head, I guess to ease the pain.

"Are you kidding me?" he said. "You stand still in this life, you get run over. C'mon! There's got to be something going on, something new you can try this year."

"Nah, it's really all the same crowd, same school, same deal. Byron is Byron, Joey's still trying to run things, Jessie is as annoying as ever, and Lauren and I are still best friends." I caught my breath for a second on that last one, thinking about Friday. But I moved on, because I didn't want to talk about it, even with Uncle James, not right then anyway. "Oh, but I've got a new teacher, though. Mr. Goldberg. That's different—I never had a guy teacher before."

Uncle James yawned a big, dramatic, bored yawn. Then he smiled and put his arm around my shoulder, leading me out to the other room. "Allow me to clue you in, Fleecy Niecey. What you're describing here is called the calm before the storm. Just when you think things are absolutely going to stay all nice and familiar, all smooth and still, all comfortable like your favorite spot on the couch that's dented perfectly to fit your *pee-goo* (that's Chinese for "butt"!), right then, at that moment when you let your guard down, that's when you get hit with the biggest change of your life."

Uncle James sighed and stood with me in the doorway as everyone gushed over Baby Zoe. "Believe me, I know." He squeezed my shoulder. "You'd better just get ready for the storm."

WATERMELON DROPPINGS

My chest felt tight as the bus doors opened on Monday morning. I wasn't sure where I would sit. I couldn't sit next to Lauren, could I?

Lauren didn't show up for her job as Bus Buddy. She was supposed to come off the bus and help me get on it, but the door opened and I saw nothing but empty steps.

There were plenty of kids at my stop who could help me up that first step, which is mostly what I needed. Until then, though, I always liked Lauren to help me more than anyone else. It was . . . comfortable. I hung out with her most of the time anyway, so getting a little help from her was no big deal. But with someone I didn't know, asking for help was like making a big announcement to everyone that I was getting weaker. So, on top of being in a big fight with my best friend, I was also feeling bad about myself. Oh, happy day.

I made it onto the bus and turned down the aisle to check out the situation. There she was, the Bus Buddy quitter, chatting with Maddie, who was sitting in *my* seat. Maddie had stolen my spot, snatched it right out from under me. I found an empty seat diagonally behind Lauren and fell into it. I watched and waited. Lauren finally turned around, but she just gave me a blank look that reminded me of a big, white sheet of paper when I can't think of anything to draw.

I didn't have a chance to talk to her through math, reading, and spelling. Finally, at lunch, I thought the tightness in my chest was going to explode through my ribcage. I couldn't take it any more. I went right over to Lauren and sat across from her.

I looked at her. She looked at me. "Why are you still mad at me?" I asked.

She chewed her sandwich slowly and then sighed, which made crumbs fly out of her mouth. This was normally something we would crack up about, but we just stared at the tiny pieces of bread.

"Arlene, you should know."

"Okay, fine. Sorry I called you a TAB. And an old lady. And feeble. Sorry."

I waited, but even after a long minute, there was nothing but silence. Finally, Lauren said one word: "Fine."

That just wasn't going to cut it. "It doesn't sound like it's fine," I said. "It sounds like you're still mad."

Lauren picked at her sandwich again and stared at it, like there were other one-word answers hidden in her ham slices. She took a deep breath and started to say what was on her mind—to her sandwich. "Well, I knew you'd be upset if I didn't want to go to horseback riding with you. I just knew it. I mean, it's like I don't ever have a choice, like I'm always supposed do everything with you. I want to help, of course, but sometimes . . . I mean, sometimes . . . it's like . . . it's like . . . it feels like I'm trapped into doing everything with you." Lauren looked up at me quickly, almost a little scared, like she just dropped a watermelon off the side of a building and was waiting for it to hit the ground and explode.

I felt like a watermelon just landed on my head. Trapped? *Trapped?!* There I go, apologizing to this girl, and she whacks me with *trapped?*

"Arlene, I'm sorry. I-I didn't mean to say that. That's not what I meant. I mean . . . I just—"

"What?!"

Lauren shook her head quickly back and forth. "Nothing. Never mind."

Talk about trapped! I felt like I'd just been slammed into a corner, no way out. What was I supposed to do here? Should I stay in this yucky place with Lauren and be miserable and lonely? Should I try to figure out how to do the whole "let's make up" thing and get rid of this tightness in my chest that was about to suffocate me? Maybe she wanted to do things with other people sometimes. I guess that was okay. But *trapped*? Really? My brain whirred like a smoothie maker, but I couldn't figure out what to do, couldn't find any words to say.

"Hey, Arlene! Lauren! What's up? What're you guys talking about? Where were you this weekend Arlene? You gonna eat those chips, Lauren?"

Byron. Thank goodness! "Hey, Byron," I said. "I went to New York to see my new cousin Zoe on Sunday. She's cute and boring all at the same time."

"Huh. Is she all red and wrinkled? Can she talk yet? Did she smell like dirty diapers?"

Like always, you have to just pick one of Byron's many questions to answer. "Byron. She's like, a month old. No, she can't talk yet."

"Huh. Does sound boring. You missed Sunday school. They showed a video, and we got popcorn and lemonade. It was all about forgiveness. Really good show. Hey, Lauren. Lauren, how 'bout those chips?"

I looked up and saw Lauren looking at me, smirking about Byron and his chatterbox mouth. I smiled too. Good ol' Byron to lighten things up. And maybe I should have seen that movie about forgiveness. Maybe that big dark cloud that dropped on us a few minutes ago would just move along outta here. Or maybe Lauren and I could escape and leave it behind.

Lauren caught my smile, and hers grew too. She threw her plastic baggie of chips toward Byron. "Enjoy."

"Thanks!" Byron ate one chip at a time, feeding them through his chomping teeth like a cartoon beaver on a log.

I enjoyed another round of smiles with Lauren, but then the bell rang to let us know lunch was officially over. We all got up to throw our stuff away and head out to the playground for recess. Byron tossed his Styrofoam tray, spork (that plastic fork/spoon combination thingie), and Lauren's plastic bag into the trash can, except that the trash can was so full that it all wobbled on top for a minute before sliding to the floor. Byron shrugged and kept walking.

I used my two hands to balance my brown bag carefully on the garbage pyramid, as if I was building a house of cards. Sheila walked toward us carrying her apple core. She stopped suddenly about ten feet away, faked right, spun left, and then with two hands over her head tossed the apple in a perfect arc dead center onto my teetering bag. The crash of the apple sent even more garbage to the floor. Sheila walked away.

"Trash goes in the trash can, Arlene, not on the floor." Oh, double happy day. It was Jessie.

"Duh. I know that, Jessie. But there's too much trash and not enough can here."

"And that's the reason you're throwing it on the floor?" Jessie's voice and eyebrows both went way up.

"I didn't throw anything on the floor. And if you're so concerned, you can help clean it up."

"Nah. Not really my problem," and with that, she swished her hair to the side and walked away from us.

Lauren shook her head and grinned. "Same old Jessie."

I smiled wide. "Yep. Nothing ever changes, does it?"

I wanted to believe that. I really did. I felt that horrible, horrible word "trapped" begin to sink slowly into the deep bottom of my memory, and I let it, hoping it would seep far enough away to drown.

Lauren and I bent to pick up the trash that had fallen after Sheila's jump shot. Where did Sheila run off to? She was the one who should have been cleaning up the mess.

"Why doesn't Greenwood recycle anyway?" asked Lauren. "Look at this. Half of what's in this pile of garbage could be taken to the recycling center."

"Good point. Maybe the SGA should do something about it." The SGA, or student government association, was a group of students who supposedly helped run the school. Seemed to me like the teachers were still in charge in the end, but at least we had a way to let them know what we thought.

"Too bad you're not still president!" Lauren said.

"Yeah. But Carlos is, and he can solve any problem. He'll figure out how to fix this. We should bring it up at the next town hall meeting."

"Sure," Lauren answered. I felt my chest loosen even more, and I took in a big breath of fresh air as we walked outside. My world seemed a little more steady. I wasn't sure exactly where I stood with Lauren, but if we kept moving forward, maybe we could roll past this whole weird argument.

BIG ACTION, BIG CHANGE

Mr. Goldberg pronounces all of his Rs. He is clearly not from around here. I heard he's from way out west. I sometimes picture him in a cowboy hat and those big chap things on his legs, and this makes me giggle to myself. But then people start looking at me like I'm crazy, and I have to stare them back down like they're crazy, and so I lose track of the whole cowboy thing.

After recess we started our "rotation," which meant social studies with Mr. Goldberg first, then science with the other fifth grade teacher Mrs. Chesterfield, and finally computer lab with Mrs. Sweeney, our librarian/computer expert. Mr. Goldberg settled us down with his smile, as always. This guy has a killer smile. It's because most of him is, like, dark: really tan skin, brown eyes, black hair that is always perfectly neat, and this dark beard-mustache thing. But then he's got these blinding white teeth. His beard-mustache thing frames this shiny smile like the night sky hugs the moon. And when he spreads his mouth into that big, bright smile, you just have to stare at him.

I've heard old people like my mother call him handsome. I don't see it. But he can get our attention, that's for sure.

"So everyone, we're going to start our presentations today." Mr. Goldberg emphasized each word, and then he clapped his hands, leaving them hanging together in the air for a moment while he said, "That's very exciting." He smirked again as he spread his hands out wide to us, like he was welcoming us into an ice cream shop offering free brownie sundaes all day. Like I said, he can really get our attention.

"I'm sure you've all been busily researching the topics you chose," he began. Whoops! I realized I hadn't even started yet! I made a mental note to get to work on my project! My presentation wasn't due until near the end of this unit, but still, I hated leaving things to the last minute. Mr. Goldberg went on, "Remember, we're presenting our reports in pairs. Today we'll hear from Carlos and Joey. But first, let's talk a minute about the point of this project. Remember, we're learning about change." Then he said softly, "Big change."

Had he been talking to Uncle James?

"Kids," Mr. Goldberg propped one foot on a small chair and rested his elbows on his knee, "think about it. Think about how we got to where we are today. Not just you and me, but *us*, our country, our society."

Joey yawned dramatically. Mr. Goldberg ignored him. "If you took a picture, a snapshot, of the way things were, say . . . two hundred years ago, and compared it to things today, these two pictures would look very, very different. For example, back then, do you know what many of you would be doing right now, in the middle of the day?"

"Feeding the dinosaurs?" Joey asked. He got a bunch of giggles out of that comment.

Mr. Goldberg did his signature smirk. "No, Joey, you're way off, time-wise. Ask Mrs. Chesterfield when the dinosaurs roamed the earth, okay Son? And report to me when you get back from science." Joey sank deeper into his seat, frowning.

"A few hundred years ago, you might not have gone to school every day." A few soft cheers bubbled up. "But I wouldn't be cheering about that. Instead of going to school, you'd be at work! And not for six hours a day like school, but for eight, ten, even twelve hours a day. Sunup to sundown! Hard work, like farming, cleaning homes, cooking, or making textiles at Slater Mill in Pawtucket." We had gone to Slater Mill for a field trip last year, on the same day as all the other elementary school kids in Rhode Island it seemed. It was a cool place, and we saw how they made cotton into cloth back in the old days.

Lauren raised her hand. "But Mr. Goldberg, I thought there were always schools for kids. Didn't we learn about the colonists last year going to little, one-room schoolhouses?"

"Great question. Yes, some kids did go to school. But—" Mr. Goldberg paused for drama, "there were no *laws* that said kids had to go to school. There was no law against forcing a child to work all day, every day. So when a law was eventually passed making rules about kids and working, huge changes had to be made. And so each of you, through your presentations, will tell us about a different law that caused big changes for our country. It's really going to be fascinating. I can't wait to—"

Ms. Farley came in just then. The wild waves in her brown hair were caught in a huge fight with the hair band trying to stretch them back into a pony-tail behind her head. This lady who called herself an occupational therapist—but really was just enemy #1 to me—stood in the doorway with her long, muscular arms crossed in front of her, and waited. As always, she seemed impatient and ready to get to work. She looked, looked, looked at me. And I just looked, looked, looked at Mr. Goldberg.

Mr. Goldberg turned to Ms. Farley and smiled his big smile. "Why, good afternoon Ms. Farley! How are you today?"

"I'm just wonderful, thank you. And how are you?"

"Fantastic!"

Then they ended their little chitchat and both looked at me—double stares going on. I looked down at my nails. I should paint them, maybe black with pink polka dots. I wondered if I could get black nail polish at the drugstore near my house.

"Arlene," Mr. Goldberg said. "I think Ms. Farley is here to see you."

"She is?" I pushed my eyebrows way up toward my hair to show how shocking this news was.

Now Ms. Farley shot a hard look at me. She knew this whole occupational therapy thing (or OT as I call it) was really getting old with me. She came to my class twice a week, sometimes to help me in the classroom and sometimes to take me to the OT room where I worked on balance and handwriting and stuff. Believe me, I'd love to stop falling so much, but it's just so weird to have this lady sit next to me in my classroom, helping me write and use scissors. It's like I'm a little preschooler or something. And sometimes, she starts helping me with my regular work, like showing me how to multiply fractions. I can do that! I'm not stupid! I just have CMT.

"Yes, Arlene, I'm here for you. Let's go. It's time for your OT session."

"But I want to hear the presentations!"

Mr. Goldberg looked at me with a hint of that sympathetic "Aww" look I've come to love and hate all at the same time. He seemed to understand that Ms. Farley's interruptions really annoyed me.

"Ms. Farley," he said, and gave her one of the super-sized, warm Mr. Goldberg smiles. "Might it be possible for Arlene to hear the student presentations? It'll take about fifteen minutes. I do think it's important for her to be here for this, since she'll be doing one in a few weeks as well."

Ms. Farley gave Mr. Goldberg this weird, giggly look. "Sure, Mr. Goldberg, if you think it's important for her, I can come back in about fifteen minutes." Then like Superman bursting out of a phone booth in his superhero uniform, her face flashed into a whole new look, and she shot this intense, not very warm at all, stare at me. "I'll be back, Arlene."

Yikes!

"So," Mr. Goldberg continued. "Carlos, Joey—you two are first. You ready?"

Carlos stood up and smoothed his shirt, tucked it in a little tighter, and walked to the front of the room. Joey jumped up and clomped behind Carlos.

"I'll start," Joey said. (No surprise there.) "I researched the—" he squinted down at his paper and began to read like the robot GPS voice in our van ("make a legal U-turn when possible"), "the National Labor Relations Act. It was passed in 1935. It gave workers the right to join unions. It said that—"

"Joey," Mr. Goldberg interrupted. "Try just talking to us. I'm going to put your report on the bulletin board later, and we can all read it. But tell us, what was it like for workers in the 1930s? We need to understand *why* a big change happened."

Joey slapped his report against his leg and looked up at us. "It stunk for workers back then. Totally stunk. It was the Great Depression, and everyone was poor and out of work. So the bosses had all the control, because if one worker didn't like the way he was treated, there were eight more who would take his place. My Gramps told me all about it. He worked totally hard, got paid like, nothing, and sometimes where he worked wasn't even safe."

"Good, Joey," said Mr. Goldberg. "Carlos, can you add to this picture?"

"Yes, I can." Carlos placed his report neatly on Mr. Goldberg's desk and raised his two hands, palms out to the class, like a king talking to his people. "I researched the California Agricultural Labor Relations Act. Like Joey said, things for workers were terrible back then in the 1930s, but for farmworkers, those terrible things continued long after that. Farmworkers suffered from things like dangerous pesticides, unfair wages, and terrible living conditions. With farm work, you're always on the move, from farm to farm. That life was really hard anyway, but they suffered even more from not being treated fairly."

"Okay," Mr. Goldberg got up and paced along the side of the classroom. "So things were very difficult for workers. But what did they do about it? What action did they take? "

Carlos answered: "The key was to join together, to organize, to form one large group so they had more power."

Mr. Goldberg clapped his hands loudly. "That's right! And what do we call it when workers do that, join together to form a group like that?"

Joey pumped his fist into the air. "Unions!"

Mr. Goldberg spoke more softly. "Bingo. Tell us more."

"Yeah, so around the time of my law," Joey said, "workers started to get together and go on strike. There was a big strike by autoworkers in Detroit and by truck drivers in Minneapolis. Then, in 1934, people who made clothes—" Joey looked down at his report, flipping papers this way and that, causing a few to drop to the floor. Finally he smacked his report with his pointer finger. "Textile workers! Yeah, textile workers went on strike, too, the largest strike ever in the country at that time. From here in Rhode Island all the way down to the south, about . . . 400,000 workers went on strike. In Woonsocket, right here in Rhode Island, there was, like, a riot."

"It was a very difficult time for everyone," Mr. Goldberg said. "So what eventually happened?"

"They passed this law, my law!" Joey explained. "The National Labor Relations Act said that it was okay for workers to form unions. Once they could do that, then they got together and worked out

ARLENE, THE REBEL QUEEN

things with the bosses, like better pay, safe conditions at work, and fair rules about hiring and stuff."

"Did it make things better?" Mr. Goldberg asked.

"Um . . . yeah, I think so," Joey said with a nod. "I did read that some people don't think unions work that well, that sometimes unions make things unfair for people who don't belong to them. But it seems like without the unions, workers didn't have any power to fix things when they were treated horribly."

"I think that's proven in my research," said Carlos. "Farmworkers were not covered by the law Joey's talking about, and so conditions never improved. I read a lot about a great leader named Cesar Chavez. His family worked on farms his whole life, and he wanted to try to make things better for farmworkers everywhere. He led strikes, too, but he also tried to get people to do boycotts."

Boycotts! Wait a minute. Uncle James was constantly talking to me about boycotts, how everyone has the power to stay away from a store or company to show them that you disagree with what they're doing.

"Cesar Chavez tried to get people all over the country to stop eating grapes."

Byron slapped his hand on his desk. "I love grapes!"

"I know, me too," said Carlos. "But the point was, if everyone stopped eating them, and the farmworkers stopped picking them, the owners of the farms would start to lose money, and they would have to work out with the farmworkers a way to be fair, to keep them safe and to make their living conditions better."

Ah, now Uncle James's boycotts made more sense. There was his boycott against the company that sold clothes made by little kids who worked in factories instead of going to school. Then there was his boycott against another company that he said polluted lakes and rivers. And of course, his boycott against the restaurant that seated a lot of other people even though we were there first. That last one seemed a little personal. I definitely needed to talk to Uncle James about this.

"So seriously, people stopped eating grapes?" Byron asked sadly.

"Well, just for a few years."

"Years?!" Byron put his head down on his desk.

"But Mr. Chavez didn't stop there. He was an amazing man. He also went on long fasts. He wouldn't eat for twenty or thirty days in order to make people pay attention to the problems for farmworkers."

Byron then fell out of his chair.

Mr. Goldberg sighed. "Unless you're on a fast right now and have fainted, Byron, get back in your chair."

Byron popped up and sat down. "Sorry, but I can't imagine not eating for a month!"

Mr. Goldberg nodded at us. "No, you're right, Byron, that is pretty dramatic action, isn't it? I mean, think about it, conditions were so bad for these workers that they made tremendous sacrifices to bring about change. Carlos, did it work for the farmworkers?"

"Well, yes. The California Agricultural Labor Relations Act of 1975 did what Joey talked about before. It gave farmworkers the right to form unions. Then with these larger farmworker groups, they were able to make conditions better for themselves and their families."

"Great work, both of you," Mr. Goldberg said. "So we see how conditions were poor for a certain group of people, in this case workers, and how when that group banded together, they gained the power they needed to make real change for the better."

"Oh, and Mr. Goldberg, I forgot to tell you the

best thing," said Carlos. "Cesar Chavez had a personal motto: '*Si se peude*,' which means, 'It can be done.'"

"It can be done," Mr. Goldberg repeated. "I like it. And it's a great way to end our first presentation, Carlos. Both of you, thank you for your hard work." Mr. Goldberg went to the front of the room and shook the hands of both Joey and Carlos in a very serious way. It was weird, but cool.

"Arlene," said an impatient voice. "You ready now? Let's go."

I covered my eyes to block the vision of Ms. Farley standing in the doorway of my classroom. I wondered how to say "OT *can't* be done" in Spanish.

TURTLE TRAP

My topic for the social studies presentation was the Americans with Disabilities Act, or the ADA. After hearing the first presentations that day, I was anxious to get going on my research. My first step: find out what Mom already knew about the topic. "Mom, you ever hear of the Americans with Disabilities Act?"

We were riding in the van after my physical therapy session, after picking up Chris from football practice. It seemed like we were always on the move, like the farmworkers Carlos talked about. Sometimes it felt like we lived in the van. It was hard to talk when we were driving because Mom's wheelchair was locked up on the passenger side, and there were no middle seats like in most vans, so I was way in back. The middle seats had been cut out because Mom needed room to turn around and move her chair into its place.

But I shouted up to my parents anyway, because really, this was the only time I had to tell them everything that was on my mind. And I usually had a lot to say. On most days, after I'd unloaded everything I'd stored up to tell my parents, Mom would prop up a thick book on two big pillows on her lap, hold the pages down with her elbows, and read to us. Even though CMT can affect a person's voice and it was hard for Mom to talk really loudly, she would strain and shout above the van noise so that Chris and I could hear her. And you know what? Chris even took out his earphones and listened. For real! Mom would read old books that she called "classics," the kind I would never pick out of the library for myself. I always got books with either lots of horses or lots of funny stuff inside. But something about Mom reading to us in the car made me want to listen.

Anyway, Mom had just finished a chapter, so I had a chance to ask her about this Americans With Disabilities Act. Turns out, like with a lot of things, Mom had an answer.

"Sure, Arlene, I've heard of the ADA. Huge deal.

I mean, I haven't read the actual law, but I read a lot about it in the newspaper when it got passed, I think maybe in 1990 or so? I was just getting out of college, I remember. It changed everything for people with disabilities. It required businesses and buses to be accessible, and it said that you can't refuse to hire someone with a disability just because they need help to do their job, like I do."

"Well, if this law was so huge," I asked, "how come we still have to walk through the back kitchen door to get in and eat at the burger place? Why did they get to keep those steps up to the front door?" Did Uncle James know about this? Shouldn't he be doing something about it?

"Good question. I'm guessing there are loopholes in the law. Why do you ask? Are you studying it at school?"

"Not exactly. We have to do a report on a big change in history, and I picked the ADA."

Mom twisted her head around as best she could to look at me—man, that must have hurt her neck. "Ooh, good. Frankly, I'd like to know more about that law myself. Might be time to raise a ruckus around town, right Hon? Get that burger place to build a ramp?" Mom pushed on Dad's shoulder and smiled. He shot a look at her out of the corner of his eye.

"Ruckus?" Dad asked. "Ah, no. That would be a no. We live in a small town, in a small state. Ruckuses make people very uncomfortable." Dad stopped the car for our weekly take-out dinner. "I'm going in to get the pizza."

"Can you get me a pizza strip too, Dad? Please?" I asked ever so politely.

"Yeah, me too, Dad," groaned Chris. He *was* alive! He had gone right to sleep after Mom finished the chapter, just pulled his hood down over his eyes and conked out.

We waited in the car while Dad ran in to get the pizza and pizza strips. Now, if you're not from around here, you may not know the difference. See, in Rhode Island, a pizza is a pizza. A pizza *strip*, though, is a long rectangle of dough with a big, thick layer of red sauce on it, sprinkled with Italian seasonings. Yes, that's right, it's basically dough and sauce. Maybe it's the type of sauce, maybe it's the seasonings, but whoo-ee, it's yummy.

Dad came back with the food, and we drove home. After we pulled into the garage, we all grabbed something—the food, workbags, school bags. Mom rode down the van's ramp, and I climbed out behind her. "Hey, Chris," I asked, "can you grab my backpack?"

He hissed out a heavy sigh, dripping with drama. "I've got my own stuff to carry, Arlene. Come on!"

Mom swerved around. "Chris, just grab it. Arlene's carrying the pizza strip bag, and your father's hands are full. Work with us here."

I followed Mom into the kitchen. "Yeah, so Mom, we have to do this whole huge report, then an oral presentation in front of the—"

Mom kept moving forward and put her book down on the kitchen table. Then she pushed through the mail with her fist. Finally, she asked, "In front of the what?"

I couldn't answer.

"Arlene," Dad asked as he came into the kitchen. "What are you doing on the floor? We washed it last Saturday."

"Funny, Dad. Real funny."

"Arlene!" Mom came over to me where I had just fallen flat on my face. I know, I have leg braces, but even so, sometimes I just lose my balance and crash down. It's really, really annoying. "Are you okay, honey?" Mom asked. "Can you get up? Here, grab my chair."

I rolled over onto my back and started to pull myself up using the arm of Mom's chair. We all usually laugh about this stuff, I think to make me feel better, and it usually works. But as I was trying to get up this day, I looked at Mom, and she looked at me. I felt connected to her in that little minute, like soul to soul. And we were both crying on the inside.

Then Dad grabbed me under my arms and lifted me up. He smoothed my hair and rested his hand on my shoulder. "I saved the pizza strips! They were safely wrapped up in the bag, totally protected, still delicious."

Mom touched my hand. "Are you okay?"

I nodded.

"What would you have done if you had your backpack on, Sweetie? It would have fallen right on top of you!"

I pictured this, and giggled a little. "No, it's so heavy, it would have made me fall backwards instead of forwards. Maybe I would have landed on my back, like on top of my backpack."

I could tell Mom was picturing this too, and she started giggling. "You'd be kind of stuck, all weighed down, wouldn't you?"

I laughed a little more. "Like a turtle on her back!"

Chris dumped my backpack at my feet. "Here, Squirt. You can repay me later. I just saved your life. You woulda been totally trapped if I hadn't carried this in, you turtle!"

Trapped. There was that word again. My laughter got sucked away like a vacuum cleaner makes a hunk of dust disappear. I felt like I couldn't breathe.

LIAR, LIAR

With the town hall meeting coming up and the garbage still overflowing the trash cans in the cafeteria, I started to look into the whole recycling issue on my own. I'd seen my mom and dad do this a lot, look up stuff on the Internet and get information. They called this their "homework." I personally was shocked that grown-ups still had to do homework, but Mom always said that you never want to show up for things unprepared. That could be a missed opportunity. I didn't really understand what she meant, but with this recycling thing, I was starting to see. If I came to the meeting armed with facts and suggestions for how we could make Greenwood more responsible to Planet Earth, I could get a lot farther than if I just shouted out that we need to get more green but had no other information.

After talking to the lady who runs the cafeteria, I found out that a ton of food was wasted every day. Kids were given stuff for lunch, whatever came with a particular menu choice, whether they wanted it or not. So they ended up throwing a lot away, like the extra roll, the celery sticks, or the apple. And of course, we threw away all sorts of plastic utensils and Styrofoam trays.

I read more on the Internet about this too, and I learned that being more responsible for our environment isn't just about recycling paper and cans. It's about really making changes. The kind of changes we were learning about in social studies class. There were so many ways we could stop using things in the first place, like all those Styrofoam trays in the cafeteria. We could have hard trays and real silverware and then just get a dishwasher so we could re-use everything. Teachers could use real coffee cups instead of those paper ones they drink from and throw away. We could put hand dryers in the bathrooms instead of using mounds of paper towels. With these changes, we could really reduce our carbon footprint, which is like the impact we have on our environment. All the fuel we use, all the stuff we throw away, it all adds to the gases that go into the atmosphere and trap in heat. This leads to climate change and temperatures on Earth rising, which is just really bad for a lot of things in nature.

Oh, I was ready for this town hall meeting (which is what our school calls a big ol' assembly) coming up in the next week. But first . . . Halloween! For as long as I could remember, I went out trick-or-treating with Lauren. But this year, she said she wasn't going out for Halloween. Yes, I know. It was very, very suspicious, especially given our fight a few weeks ago. My mind raced like a dog chasing his tail, around and around trying to figure out what it meant. Was it because of me that Lauren didn't want to go out for Halloween? I wasn't even sure what was going on between us. Were we still best-friends-forever, or just plain-old-best-friends? Maybe we were kind of like, past-best-friends-who-still-got-along? Or past-best-friends-who-had-a-fight-and-never-really-made-up-but-who-aren't-being-totally-mean-to-each-other-at-the-moment? It was so confusing!

How would I figure out why Lauren wasn't going trick-or-treating with me?

"Lauren," I said, "why aren't you going out trick-or-treating with me?" (Generally, I don't see any way to get an answer you need other than to just ask the question.)

My mother and I had gone to Lauren's house to drop off something for the PTA meeting coming up, and of course, our moms were chatting like PTA people always do, so that left Lauren and me just standing in her driveway. But I didn't mind at all, because it was hard to find a minute when Lauren was alone at school. I didn't want to ask her around other people because it could be embarrassing. I mean, what if she answered, "Because I'm not really your best friend anymore?"

Lauren looked startled by this question. *Well, too bad*, I thought. *If you're going to break a five-year pattern, you'd better expect someone to ask you about it.*

"Um . . . I don't know," Lauren shrugged. "I just don't feel like trick-or-treating this year. I'm kinda . . . like, over it, you know? I'm going to be eleven in a few months. It feels babyish to be dressing up, ringing doorbells, collecting candy."

I stared at her. "Are you calling me a baby?"

"No! I mean, I can totally see why you would

want a bunch of candy. I'm just saying I don't want to go. It's just me, just my thing."

"Yeah, sure, whatever." I looked up at the clouds to see if that dark one was creeping back toward us again. Of course, this made me lose my balance and wobble backwards. I held my arms out and steadied myself. "Okay," I said. "Well, Mom and I have to get to the store. Gotta go pick out a costume. You know, before the little kids buy them all up." I shouldn't have said that last thing, I know. But I was feeling hurt, really hurt by this whole thing with her.

"Arlene, I'm sorry! I just don't want to go out trick-or-treating. I'm not calling you a baby."

"Uh-huh. I heard you. Gotta go. Bye."

Lauren looked worried. But I didn't believe her story. I truly didn't. Look, if there's one thing I was born with, besides messed-up nerves from CMT, it was a good gut. That's what my grandfather always told me. He'd say, "Arlene, you gotta listen to your gut. When something just doesn't feel right, it probably ain't right. And from what I see, young lady, you got a good gut in you, right about . . . here!" And then he'd tickle me like crazy.

It was probably just an excuse to tickle me, now that I think about it. But this idea has really worked for my whole life, so far. I try to do things that make sense, things that feel right to me. If I spend too much time thinking, thinking, thinking about something, I feel all lost and stressed out. So I try to keep in mind what Grandpa said to me, and I try to do what my gut tells me to do.

When Lauren said all of a sudden that she's not doing Halloween, yes, something just didn't feel right to me. But what could I do? I asked her about it, and she had answered. I couldn't accuse her of flat-out lying. But my gut was screaming, "Liar, liar, liar!"

I tried to enjoy Halloween though, even without Lauren. I went with Byron, which was a ton of fun actually. He raced from house to house, like any good pirate would, without ever stopping to catch a breath. He waved his sword and yelled "Boo-ya!" to everyone we passed. My crazy friend made up a different greeting at each house. "Trick or treat! Smell our feet! Give us something good to eat!" That one was pretty standard, but then he got better. "Trick or treat! We can't be beat! We're the scariest kids on your street!" or "Trick or treat! You can't compete! We'll scare you right into next week!" And when he ran out of words that rhymed with "treat," he switched it around. "Treat or trick! We're first pick! Give us candy 'til we get sick!"

At one point, though, I couldn't keep up. My legs just couldn't walk anymore, and my ghost sheet was threatening to trip me. Luckily we were back near Byron's house, having made a complete circle around the neighborhood. Byron convinced his dad to drive us over to another neighborhood, for one last streak of trick-or-treating. But I had to wait in the car because I was so wiped out. I had done my best to keep up with Bryon. But he was the absolute trick-or-treat champion.

He ran up to each house in the other neighborhood and explained that he had a great ghost-friend in the car and could he please have extra candy for her? More suspicious neighbors squinted out toward the car, straining to see if Byron was really telling the truth or just trying to get extra candy. I rolled down the window and waved, calling, "Hey there!" to help Byron prove his case. "She's got two broken legs," he told a few people. For one really suspicious old guy I stuck one leg out the car window. The whole thing could have been totally embarrassing, but Byron and I laughed so much about it that it all felt okay in the end.

Until I saw her. There was Lauren, walking with Maddie in this other neighborhood. I only saw them from the car window as we were driving home, but I was completely sure it was her.

How dare she! She lied to me, betrayed me, abandoned me, left me in the dust, kicked me when I was down, walked me to the edge of a cliff and shoved me over the side yelling "Timber!" as I plunged to my death. She lied right to my face.

My brain and heart joined my gut in a big chorus concert, singing, "Liar, liar, liar!"

ACTION PLAN

When it was time for the town-hall meeting that next week, I still could barely stand to be in the same room with Ms. Liar Pants. I hadn't talked to her since Halloween, and I wasn't planning to until . . . well, frankly, I never would. She tried to talk to me in school that week, but I just nodded and walked away. I wouldn't speak to her. I couldn't speak to her. I felt that if I did, my feelings would blow her over as they gushed out of my mouth with the force of water from a fire hose.

At the meeting, Lauren brought up the idea about recycling more at Greenwood. I said nothing. Carlos and the SGA thought this was a great idea for a service project, and anyone interested in working on it was supposed to meet after school in the library. I figured I'd go and, once again, say nothing to you-know-who.

Mrs. Sweeney, our librarian and the teacher in charge of the SGA, ran the after-school meeting. That was a good thing because like Mr. Goldberg, she is someone who can get attention, although in a really different way. She is very short, very wide, and very strong. I once saw her lift a whole stack of humongous books that another teacher had rolled in on a cart. Mrs. Sweeney just stuck her hands underneath the pile, sucked in a breath, and, whoosh, lifted the whole bunch up. Then she pushed the cart away with a little karate sidekick, grumbling, "Get this roly-poly thing outa my library!"

After school at the meeting, Mrs. Sweeney leaned back, crossed her arms, and read out loud our action plan that she had written on a big white board with a dry-erase marker. Our committee had been sitting in the library for over an hour, since just after the final school bell rang, and Mrs. Sweeney looked about ready to call it a day.

"All right, this'll do it," Mrs. Sweeney said to no one in particular. "So, we meet with Mr. Musgrove to get his approval, start an awareness campaign, and see what happens. Fine. Sounds good."

Joey stood up. "But where's the action in this action plan?"

Mrs. Sweeny let her puffy arms fall to her side and slap her wide hips with a thwap. "There's plenty of action here! You're going to present your ideas to the principal—action number one. Then, you're going to educate everyone about why we need to save our planet. That's action number two. Then you're going to put some more bins out, try to get everyone to recycle more paper and plastic water bottles and things. Boom, boom, boom. There's a whole heap of action here, Joey." Mrs. Sweeney looked sadly up at the clock on the wall.

Joey shook his head in disgust. "Just sounds like a lot of talkin' to me. You know, back when workers were being treated unfairly, people had strikes and boycotts and things."

"Yeah," said Sheila. "This is not really very exciting."

Joey threw his hands toward the ceiling. "We should boycott school! Student strike! Strike, strike, strike!" Joey tried to get a chant going in the room. But he forgot Mrs. Sweeney was in charge.

Mrs. Sweeney threw her arms across her broad chest and crossed them firmly. "Joey Dangerfield!

Knock it off before your strike turns into detention! Now, people! This is an *action* plan, not an *entertainment* plan. You want excitement and drama, go be in the school play."

"But Mrs. Sweeney," I asked, "what if we do all this talking, and nobody ever really makes any changes?"

Lauren spoke up, in a quiet voice that sounded even a bit shaky. "They *will* if we do a good job educating them. If they do nothing, then that's our fault."

I turned my head to look at her slowly, stiffly, like one of those mechanical Santa statues whose head creaks back and forth with a pasted-on smile. I answered my ex-best-friend in a quiet voice too, but tried hard to smooth out any shakiness. "All I'm saying is . . . sometimes, it takes more than a bunch of talking to make people do something. We need to plan what we're going to do if nothing really changes."

"We need Trash Police maybe," Sheila said. "And they can write tickets to anyone caught throwing away plastic bottles."

"Ooh, yeah," shouted Joey. "And if they still won't recycle, we'll arrest them. My cousin can get us handcuffs. He's a cop in New Jersey."

Mrs. Sweeney just stood with tight fists on her hips. "Joey, Sheila. You guys really need to join the school play. Enough complaining! This is our action plan. Frankly, we're done here. I'll set up a meeting with Mr. Musgrove for early next week so we can get his approval."

Byron raised his hand. "Who's going to talk to Mr. Musgrove? When will the meeting be? I could do it. Me and Mr. Musgrove are tight!"

Mrs. Sweeney impatiently looked around the room at her choices. "Well, it's certainly not gonna be Brad Pitt and Angelina Jolie over there," she said, nodding toward Joey and Sheila. "We need calm, reasonable people. Lauren, Arlene—you two are going."

My stiff, Santa head suddenly loosened and shook violently. "No! No, Mrs. Sweeney. That's not going to work!"

Lauren stammered too. "No . . . I . . . I don't think . . . um . . . I'm not going to—"

"We are done here!" Mrs. Sweeney repeated, to the ceiling.

I didn't want to look at Lauren, but I wanted to see how she looked. So I squinted toward her. She looked shaky. Good. As queen of Fakedom County, she should be crumbling under the weight of her liar crown.

After the meeting we all headed down the hallway to get on the late bus or wait for our parents to pick us up. Lauren was way ahead of me, with lots of distance in between, just the way I needed it. Jessie, however, was right beside me.

"Whoa, Arlene, what is going on with you and Lauren? Why are you all mad at her?"

"Who said I was mad at her?"

"Come on, Arlene. First of all, I heard from Maddie that you're mad at Lauren. And then I saw it myself, just now. There's no denying it. I just want to know why."

"Why would I tell you? It's my private business."

"So you guys *are* in a fight! Maddie and Izzy were right. I knew it!"

I stopped walking so I could give Jessie a hard stare. "What do you mean, Maddie and Izzy? Why is everyone talking about me? Why doesn't everyone mind their own business?"

"You put it out there, Arlene. Besides, we all know you and Lauren. You think we don't see what's going on? You guys have been best friends forever, and now you're clearly not. Maybe Lauren's just getting tired of you." Jessie shrugged. "It happens."

And with that, Jessie tightened her hair in her hair-band and walked away from me.

I leaned against the wall and bent forward a little, because it felt like someone had just kicked me in my gut, which seemed to be getting me into a lot of difficult situations lately. Kids kept passing me, but I didn't even see them. My mind was racing again, round and round. I was still so mad at Lauren, but I couldn't deal with what Jessie had said. How could Jessie know what was behind all this? Could she possibly be right? Was Lauren just tired of being my friend?

DIVIDED HIGHWAY

Mrs. Sweeney scheduled the meeting with Mr. Musgrove the very next week. I figured he'd be booked up for months and I could put this horrible meeting off until doomsday. But whoa, here was doomsday, all up in my face.

I still hadn't talked to Lauren, but now it was less from anger and more from wanting to ignore this whole messy mess. At the meeting time, it was like mirror images: Lauren and I approached Mr. Musgrove's office from opposite ends of the hallway, saw each other, and then both slowed to a crawl, inching our way into his office. We turned to stand side by side and face our principal, looking like a united team but feeling like a divided highway.

"Arlene, how nice to see you again. How's this

year going for you, young lady?" Mr. Musgrove twinkled at me from behind his big, shiny glasses.

"Great, Mr. Musgrove. Just great." I meant my answer to be kind of sarcastic, but he didn't seem to notice.

"Lauren, good to see you, too," Mr. Musgrove said. "You girls have been pretty much attached at the hip since kindergarten. Such a beautiful friendship!"

"Hmm, yeah. Beautiful," I mumbled. Now that *must* have come out sarcastic.

Lauren got right to the point. She probably didn't want to be there any longer than I did. "Mr. Musgrove, we're here to talk to you about the SGA's plan to reduce Greenwood's carbon footprint. We must do more to save our planet. We throw away a ton of recyclables, and we waste way too much. We've got to do better and—"

"So we've got to take action," I interrupted. "We're going to put recycling bins all over the cafeteria, in the hallway, in every classroom. We'll need to schedule a weekly pick-up from the local recycling plant in town. And we should think about getting rid of all the plastic forks and things in the cafeteria—"

"Actually, what we really want to do is raise *awareness*," Lauren cut me off, like we were in some kind of interruption contest. "We'll make posters, give presentations to the classes, and really get people to participate in this mission. Once people know how much difference we can make with just a few changes, the rest will fall into place."

"But of course," I said, raising my voice to make sure I drowned out Lauren, "if we need to, we'll have to really push for change. Like I really think we need to rework the whole system in the cafeteria, maybe buy a dishwasher, change the way we serve the food to reduce waste—"

"Whoa, whoa," Mr. Musgrove held up his hand to me. I was shocked. First of all, did we invite him to be in our interruption contest? I didn't think so. Second of all, was he actually giving me the "talk-to-the-hand" sign? How rude!

"Girls," Mr. Musgrove continued. "Slow down. I'm with you on the awareness thing, but not so much on things like the purchase of a dishwasher for the cafeteria. We've got a budget, and we've got to stick to it. There's no money for dishwashers, deliveries to the recycling center, and such things. We recycle what the town will pick up, and there's a limit to that. That's about all we can do. I like your idea of raising awareness though. That sounds like a very worthy project for the SGA."

"But that won't change anything," I said. "What's the point?"

"Arlene, you changed a lot of things around this school last year, and all for the better. But we're in a different position now. We have no extra money this year. Changing attitudes may be all you can do at this point. With increased awareness, people will do what they can, maybe bring less plastic from home, that kind of thing. The school can't lay out any money for this project."

"Sounds good, Mr. Musgrove," Lauren said. "Thanks for your support."

My mouth just hung open.

"Anytime, girls. Anytime."

I wanted to burst out of the office with a whoosh and a slam of the door, but of course, I can't burst out of anything anymore with these leg braces. It took all my strength to just stay on my feet, never mind bursting. So I wobbled out, put my hand against the wall for balance, and whirled around toward Lauren as best I could.

"What was that all about?! 'Thanks for your support?' Support for what? Support for a bunch of talking, blah-blah-blah-ing. No action. No change. No difference!"

"Arlene! I didn't mean to . . . I just said what we talked about at the meeting."

"No, you just sold us out. You caved!"

"I just . . . what else could we do Arlene?"

"We could stand up for what we believe in!"

"I am! Just because I don't want to boycott the school or create a Trash Police force, you think I don't believe in this cause? We came up with this idea together, remember?"

Lauren looked like she was about to cry. This was about more than recycling and Mr. Musgrove. Of course, this made tears fill my eyes too. I don't cry often, but seeing someone else cry is like turning on my tear faucet.

Lauren looked down at the floor then back up at me. Her voice was shaky. "Why are you so mad at me? Why are we fighting again?"

"Are you serious? How do you not know?" I took a step back from her. "You lied to me, Lauren. Lied right to my face." Then I leaned in, so she could see the face that she lied right to.

Now it was Lauren's turn to back up. Almost in fear it seemed. "About Halloween?"

"Yes! About Halloween! How did you think that would make me feel, huh?"

Lauren squeezed her eyes shut for a second, and

then opened them again. "I didn't lie to you! I really wasn't going out for Halloween. But then Maddie came to my house to trick-or-treat, and she asked if I wanted to walk around her neighborhood for a little bit. She was almost done. We went to, like, five houses. It was no big deal."

Okay, I had to think about this. Could this be true?

"Arlene," Lauren said, "I didn't lie to you. I just didn't want to go trick-or-treating this year. I don't know. It was like, I do the same thing for Halloween every year. I do the same thing all the time. I felt like doing something different, staying home this time, passing out the candy. I never meant to hurt your feelings. I hate that we're fighting. I've felt horrible these past few weeks, just horrible."

Well, I felt awful too. Anger doesn't feel good to me. I think I shine much better when I'm happy. Plus, it could be true that Maddie invited her for Halloween at the last minute.

I could end this right here, I thought, *and have things back to normal again.*

"I'm not really having the time of my life here either," I said. "But really, it felt like you lied to me."

"I didn't, Arlene. I swear, I didn't. I was telling

the truth when we talked about Halloween. But then things changed."

I shrugged. "Okay. Okay, I guess."

I felt a relief that surprised me, a relief that I must have really needed. This up-and-down, now-we're-friends-now-we're-not thing with Lauren was really stressing me out. The idea that this could all be over was like that first bite into a thick, rich chocolate bar on Halloween night—ahhh!

We both stood there together for a minute. Maybe she was feeling as relieved as me.

"Okay," I broke the silence. "What about this recycling plan? We may need to do more than raise awareness. The school's going to have to spend some money if we're going to really make a difference."

"Let's figure that out later. Believe me, I want this to work just as much as you do. Let's go make some posters and get going on the first step in our plan."

Well, I couldn't argue with that. Maybe that dark cloud would pass us once again, at least for the moment. We would work on some posters, get back on track.

But I really felt like we were in for more resistance from Mr. Musgrove than we thought. After

just ending this awful fight with Lauren, I wasn't
sure I had the energy for another big battle!

9

UNITED WE STAND

On the Tuesday before Thanksgiving, everyone's mood was light and fluffy. It would be a half-day on Wednesday, and nobody was doing all that much work in class. It was Turkey Day in the cafeteria, of course, and kids gobbled down their Thanksgiving preview with energy and excitement.

I walked through the cafeteria and found my table—the one with Byron, Sheila, Carlos, Jessie, Joey, and Lauren. Things with Lauren and me still felt a little strange, but we weren't really concentrating on that because we were distracted by the holiday season and all the other stuff going on.

While we were gobbling our food, Jessie turned to throw her napkin into the trash can at the end of the table. "Eww!" she cried, and scooted away from it, pushing Byron over on the long bench. Byron then fell into Sheila, and, like dominoes, everyone on the bench got bumped by the person next to them.

The can must not have been emptied after the last lunch, and it was completely overflowing. A piece of turkey was sliding through oozing gravy along the bottom of a Styrofoam tray, like a sled down a slushy slope. "That is just disgusting," Jessie said and shook her head.

"It sure is," Carlos said. "Lauren, what are we doing about the recycling stuff? The posters around school don't seem to be doing anything."

"Well," Lauren said, "it probably hasn't been enough time. Maybe we need to talk to Mr. Musgrove again."

"Talking isn't going to do anything!" Sheila said. "I thought we had an action plan? We need to *do* something!"

"Sheila's right," Carlos said. "Think about the kinds of sacrifices we learned about in social studies, the things that Cesar Chavez went through to create change. A bunch of posters won't make any difference!"

"I mean, I simply can't look at this anymore,"

Jessie moaned. "At least get more trash cans. Or empty them once in a while!"

"No," I said. "It's not about more trash cans. It's about not wasting food! Just use what we need and no more. I mean, really, how hard would it be to just give people the amount of food they're going to eat? Or just use trays we can wash and reuse?"

"We've got to take a stand!" shouted Sheila. "Come on, people, let's do this. Let's do this right now! Let's protest! Let's take action! Ooh, maybe we can get arrested! I'm ready to go to jail for the cause!"

"You wouldn't go to jail," Joey interjected. "You'd go to juvenile detention!"

"I'm not getting sent to juvie right before Thanksgiving," Jessie held up her hand to our faces. "My aunt is making homemade macaroni and cheese, and that is the best in the world. No way am I eating prison food instead of mac and cheese!"

"Oh please!" Sheila said with disgust. "You and your mac and cheese. This is about justice! We will not back down! We will not give in!" Sheila pumped her fist into the air.

"Yeah! We will not give in!" Byron pumped his fist next to Sheila's. It was like an invitation. Who could resist?

"We will stand together, in unity!" I shouted and

pumped my fist into the air, reaching out for Sheila's arm to steady myself.

Byron whispered in my ear, "We'll get to eat right? We'll still get to eat Thanksgiving dinner?"

"You people don't know how to handle yourselves with law enforcement. I'd better stick around. Count me in!" Up went Joey's fist.

Jessie put her fist together with ours, although without any pumping. "I'm with you, because this is just too disgusting. But understand: I'm *not* going to jail with you and miss Thanksgiving."

Carlos raised his hand slowly and closed his eyes. "It can be done," he said like a pastor saying a prayer on Sunday morning.

That left Lauren. There went that worried look of hers, as always. She looked at me, right at me. Then she shook her head. "No," she said. "I'm not going to." And she slowly walked away.

"Okay, that's cool, that's fine," Sheila said. "That's up to her. Whatever. Let's do this after school. Let's just take down some of those posters and march in front of the school today while the buses are loading, get everyone's attention."

"Yeah! And we'll need a chant, a rhyme," Byron said. "Protestors always chant. Arlene, we can make that up. Me and you. We're good at that. Come on, during recess we'll come up with stuff."

"Cool," I said. This was going to be awesome!

"Okay," Sheila said. "Let's all grab a poster on the way out to the buses, and Byron and Arlene will lead us in chants as we march the sidewalks today! Let's do this people—we owe it to Mother Earth!" She shoved her fist into the air again. "One more time!" And we all punched the air together.

We were going to make change happen!

Of course, my gut couldn't help but whisper, *Psst, change creates more change. Look out!*

RALLY TIME

"We're here!" Byron shouted.

"To say!" I screamed.

"That Mother Earth is in de-cay!" Carlos scolded (kind of like my dad!).

"And so!" I shouted.

"We know!" Jessie yelled back.

"We must act to save her soul!" we all roared.

I led our line, pumping our posters into the air, shouting our message to the growing crowd. The buses at Greenwood wait for students in these long, diagonal parking spots along a wide sidewalk in front of the school. Parents also gather outside the "walker door," which is on the left side of the school, where all those kids who walk home come busting out at dismissal. And then there's the carpool loop, on the right side of the school, where cars line up to drive kids home. So this whole area of the sidewalk and front lawn around the flagpole was like a busy train station, with kids, bus patrols, teachers, and parents hustling and bustling, the perfect spot to do our thing: stage a good ol' rally in front of lots of people.

As our protest gathered steam, the chaos of the scene began to disappear, and like a wave in a football stadium, the crowd all turned toward us and began to listen. We had everyone's attention. That was when Byron and I stepped it up!

Byron: "Mother Earth is dying! People will be crying!"

Me: "We waste what she's supplying! We've got to stop denying!"

Byron: "We've got to take a stand, demand a better plan!"

Me: "Listen all of you, for a clue on what to do!"

Then we all began to clap and chant, "Re-duce! Re-use! Re-cycle!" Over and over we chanted, until a whole bunch of people joined in. The noise was incredible. I felt powerful and strong. Our voices filled the air, and like a gust of Rhode Island ocean wind, our shouts whooshed throughout the crowd. Soon even neighbors from houses across the street stepped out of their front doors to watch. Like the textile workers of Woonsocket, or the farmworkers of California, we were reaching people with our ideas. Forget some dumb poster stuck on a wall in a hall next to the gym. No, this was how you made change. This was powerful.

And then, suddenly, it disappeared. Kids turned their backs to us and started to get on buses again. Teachers hustled students along the sidewalk. Neighbors went back into their houses. Parents reached for their kids' hands and began walking home. I looked back and forth and all around to figure out why, what had happened. And then I saw Mr. Musgrove, his big shoes clomping along the sidewalk, baby blue tie flying out to the side of his neck from his high-speed march toward us.

He took humongous steps over to our little group so that he was towering over us in like, two seconds. "What is going on here? Stop this, right now!" He looked quickly at our signs. "Reduce, recy—what in the world?" Then he looked quickly at me. "Arlene! What is going on?"

"Um, hi there, Mr. Musgrove."

His eyes narrowed at me. "I believe we talked about this a few weeks ago, and I believe we made a plan. This was not in our plan."

"I know, but Mr. Musgrove—"

"I don't want to hear it."

"But can I just say—"

"Arlene! You came to my office to talk about recycling, and we agreed to posters and nothing more. Never was there any mention of riots or ruckus on my sidewalk! And at dismissal time!"

I laughed at the word "ruckus." It made me think of Mom's comment to Dad about making a ruckus over not being able to get into the burger place because of the stairs.

Mr. Musgrove suddenly leaned down and shoved his face until it was like, an inch away from my own, right into my personal-space bubble. "Arlene!" he shouted. "This is *not a joke!*"

Whoa! I started to sweat. Where were my peeps? Where was my backup?

"But we're just walking to our buses and talkin' and rhymin'," Joey piped in. "What's the big deal?"

Mr. Musgrove pointed a long, bony finger at Joey. "You, young man, hardly need any more trouble."

Sheila spoke up too. "I mean, we do have the right to free speech, don't we?"

Mr. Musgrove folded his arms across his chest as his face reddened to the color of strawberries. He spoke with a hiss, through clenched teeth, trying to control his boiling anger like someone struggling to stuff a jack-in-the-box back into its box. "You have the *right* to get on that bus and go home. And that's *it*. Or get to my office so I can call your parents! Make your choice and MOVE!"

Now I was not only sweating but shaking too. I looked at Byron, Sheila, Carlos, Joey, and Jessie. They looked back at me and at each other. Nobody moved. I think maybe Carlos and Joey's presentation was still fresh in our minds, or maybe the spirits of the protestors from history had camped out in our bodies. For whatever reason, nobody moved.

"I said, NOW!" Mr. Musgrove said, this time pretty much screaming at us.

Whoa, okay. I was ready to call it quits. But I didn't want to be the first to give in. I probably gave everyone else a good, old-fashioned Lauren look—all worried and scared. Actually, everyone else looked a little scared too.

I had to do the safe thing here. I silently turned and walked toward my bus. I glanced back and like little sheep, the rest of the group quietly walked to the buses, carpools, wherever they were supposed to go.

And then I began to breathe again. Whew!

I got to the steps of my bus and looked up that

mountain of stairs. Of course, Lauren wasn't there. She wasn't at the protest, and she wasn't there to help me now. I saw her, though, looking out the window at me, probably too scared to help for fear of getting in trouble along with us ruckus makers. I swear I saw her shake her head a little. I grabbed the railing with two hands and heaved myself up the steps of the bus.

Mrs. Kracken craned her head upward to search the rearview mirror, shouting, "Hey! Whe-ah's Ah-lene's help-ah?"

"I don't need any help," I mumbled between heavy breaths as I reached the top of the stairs. "Don't need any help at all."

DRAMATIC!

I focused on that steak knife, pretending I was a superhero who could shoot fiery laser beams at objects and move them with the power of my mind. *You will obey me*, I thought.

Nothing happened.

Stupid knife.

I was in charge of cutting up the carrots, celery, peppers, and broccoli for our vegetable appetizer plate before Thanksgiving dinner. I really like chopping things, and I know it's good for my fingers to keep them working. Okay, it was a little bit like occupational therapy on a holiday, but as I created a sliced-veggie circle around the edge of the platter, I couldn't help feeling a little bit proud.

But after a while, the knife stopped cooperating

in our mission. It was going its own way. I strained my fingers to hold the knife tightly and guide it along the celery for a nice, even slice. While I was very careful like Dad had shown me and didn't cut off any fingers, I couldn't get the knife to do the right thing. My celery sticks were looking more like celery chunks. And my fingers were red and white and deformed from pressing up against the knife handle.

I put down my tool and shook my hand like a jazz dancer to get the blood flowing again. Chris walked behind my chair and reached over my head, grabbing a handful of freshly cut pepper slices. Then he dunked them into the sauce and dripped dip all over my perfect vegetable circle.

"Hey! Get your paws outa my veggies," I yelled.

"I need energy," Chris smiled, and he went back to the other end of the dining room table where he was in charge of peeling potatoes.

"Then eat a potato," I said.

"I can't eat it raw! It must be cooked and mashed and seasoned to perfection."

"Just mash it with your teeth and throw some salt on your tongue. You'll be all set."

"If you would just keep chopping and stop talking, Samurai Sister, then I could have a snack and we'd still have enough left over for the appetizer plate."

"Oh, I'll keep chopping, but it won't be vegetables!" I warned and shook the knife at him.

"Don't slice up your brother, Arlene," Dad said calmly as he walked through the dining room carrying an armful of fancy dishes. "And Chris, I'd prepare for a duel, just in case."

I giggled and got ready to start chopping again, but then Uncle James sat down at the table beside me, running his hand through his dark, spiky hair. I was so happy Uncle James had made the trip to see us for the holiday.

"Holy cannoli. Your cousin will not go to sleep. I mean, who doesn't want to take a nap? Do you know what I would give for a nap?"

"Well, why don't you take one?" I asked.

Uncle James was already tapping an email or text or something on his phone. "No time, Teeney Leeney, no time."

"Want a carrot stick?" I asked him.

"Oh, yeah!" Uncle James took a big bite, munched hard, and then held the rest of the stick in the corner of his mouth like a cigar. Then he put down his phone and stared at me, with the same laser-beam look I was just giving to these vegetables. After a moment he popped the carrot out of his mouth and asked, "How you doing, girl?"

I put down my knife and gave him a big stare back. "I've been waiting to tell you! We've been learning in social studies about all these laws that made big changes in our country, like when people don't have equal rights and stuff. Isn't that what you do for your job?"

"Sort of. What are you learning about exactly?"

"Well, so far some kids reported on Cesar Chavez and workers' rights. But we've got a lot more presentations coming up, and I'm supposed to do one on the Americans with Disabilities Act."

"Ah, the ADA," Uncle James said as he sat back and waved his carrot stick in the air. "Really interesting law. It held a lot of promise, but there's a lot of work still to be done if you ask me."

"But let me tell you the best part. So, we're trying to get the school to do more recycling and stuff. You know, be more green. And just like the textile workers of Woonsocket and Cesar Chavez in California, we marched in front of the school with signs, chanting about why we need to change what we're doing."

Uncle James threw his carrot on the table, leaned toward me, and grabbed both my shoulders. "What?

You held a protest? Are you kidding me?" He slapped the table hard. "Now *that's* what I'm talkin' about!"

"It was so cool, Uncle James! We chanted and marched, and then our principal told us to stop because we were being disruptive to the dismissal process."

Now Uncle James was on the edge of his seat, leaning on its front legs so the back legs were up in the air. Just the kind of position that would get me yelled at. But I guess that's what you get to do when you're an adult, a really awesome adult.

"That's just like the Man!" Uncle James punched his palm with his fist. "Always shutting down protests and suffocating the truth. So, you got stopped before you even got started, huh?"

"Well, we almost kept going. At first, when Mr. Musgrove told us to stop, we tried to talk to him about it. We almost didn't follow his direction to get on the bus."

Uncle James let the back legs of his chair fall onto the floor with a bang, and he leaned back in his chair, like he was totally wiped out from this shocking news story. He shook his head and smiled a huge smile. "My little Spunky Monkey. Are you serious? You almost said no to your principal?"

I looked right into his eyes and I could see that

he got it, that he was proud of me. My own huge smile was stretching my cheeks so much they hurt!

A loud baby wail pierced this great moment between me and my uncle. "James!" Aunt Marie called from the kitchen. "The baby! Can you see what she needs? My hands are all up in the turkey!"

"Marie!" Uncle James shouted over his shoulder without turning away from me. "Arlene and I are talking. I'll get her. In a second!" He leaned toward me and said softly, "So, okay. Then what happened?"

"Well, we all kinda got scared. So we got on our buses and went home."

He nodded and sighed. "Yeah, I understand. This was your first time, your first experience with social protest. Next time Mr. Muskrat decides to stomp on your Constitutional rights, you'll be ready."

"Well, what should we do next time?" I definitely needed some help here. I saw no other way out of that situation.

The baby wailing continued, but Uncle James waved his hands and kept talking. "Okay, so you did the straightforward kind of protest—chanting, signs, and all that. But there are lots of different ways to take action, to make your point. It's all about getting people's attention. If you read about Cesar Chavez, then you know the power he created with his fasting and boycotts."

"James!" Aunt Marie shouted, and I heard her stomp her foot on the kitchen floor. "Get your daughter!"

Uncle James stood up, flopped his arms against his sides, and huffed out a loud sigh. "Marie!" he shouted back. "I'm going!" Then he stomped around the dining room table toward the hall, still yelling. "I needed to finish talking to Arlene! Zoe's not going anywhere, my GOSH!"

Uncle James turned and winked at me. "Sometimes, you just gotta be *dramatic*," he whispered.

POWERFUL CHANGE

Back at school after Thanksgiving, Mr. Goldberg clapped his big, tan hands together and smiled his toothy smile. "I'm so excited," he said smoothly, like spreading frosting on a cake. "Today we hear from Byron and Sheila on their social studies reports. Let's give them a hand, shall we?"

We pelted them with booming applause, and Byron and Sheila worked the crowd like they were celebrities on a red carpet. "Thank you, thanks, thank you," Byron said as he swayed up to the front of the class. Sheila raised her hand to the ceiling as if to shield herself from paparazzi camera flashes. When they both reached the chalkboard, though, they stopped suddenly, spun around and faced the class. We stopped clapping immediately, confused by this weird and sudden move. Then they both put their hands on their hips and shot military stares at us, a company of new, raggedy recruits.

"I'm here to tell you about the Civil Rights Act of 1964," Byron said. "This was a legendary law that African-Americans like me had to wait over a hundred years for."

"And I'm here to tell you about the 19th Amendment that gave women the right to vote," Sheila said as she stepped in front of Byron, almost giving him a little shove to the side. "Talk about waiting! Hundreds of years we slaved away in the colonies, and we never had any say in anything!"

"Talk about slaves!" Byron moved in front of Sheila. Those two looked like they were doing some kind of dance routine at this point. "Black people were dragged to this country from Africa to be just that: slaves!"

We all wanted in on this variety show thing going on between Byron and Sheila. We started shouting out comments, generally making a lot of noise.

"Guys, guys," Mr. Goldberg said. "Keep it down, now. Byron and Sheila worked hard to make this an interesting and informative presentation, but you're going to have to be a fantastic audience in order to learn from it."

"Mr. Goldberg," Sheila said, holding up her hand like a crossing guard stopping traffic, "I'd appreciate it if you didn't refer to me, or my fellow sisters, as 'guys.' If you hadn't noticed, this class is made up of women and boys. Please. Watch your labels."

Mr. Goldberg fought off the smirk that tried to creep onto his face as he shook his head at Sheila. She kept her military stare directed right between his eyes. "No offense intended," he said, nodding respectfully toward Sheila. "Like we planned, Byron, why don't you go first, and then we'll hear a full report from Sheila."

"Sure thing," said Byron, and he turned to face the class, spreading his hands out wide toward us, like a mini Mr. Goldberg. "My friends, my story doesn't start in 1964 when the Civil Rights Act was passed. No, we need to go back in time, back hundreds of years when black people were forced to be slaves. Kids like me were ripped away from their parents and sold to white families far away, like we were an old couch or something."

I pictured a kid looking just like Byron—deep brown skin, shaved head, big smiling eyes, constant grin—being yanked away from his parents' outstretched hands. I shuddered.

"But then, even after slavery ended,

African-Americans were still treated unfairly. A lot of states made all these rules about how if you were black, you couldn't go to this school, you couldn't swim in this pool, you couldn't drink from this bubbler.[1] Even when people tried to change these rules, it didn't work. This one guy, Homer Plessy, took his case to court. He had been arrested for sitting in the whites-only car on a train." Byron paused to look straight into our eyes. "And the Supreme Court of the United States said that it was fine to arrest a guy for sitting in the wrong seat on a train. They said that having separate places for blacks and whites was okay as long as they were 'equal.'" Byron slammed his fist into Mr. Goldberg's desk. "But separate isn't equal."

The class was completely silent. We had never seen Byron this serious. I held my hands out in front of me. Byron, my little friend from across the street, was radiating power.

"So," Mr. Goldberg said quietly, "it sounds like things were pretty bad for African-Americans in this country by the 1950s and 60s. What did they do to bring about change like the Civil Rights Act?"

"Well, lots of people protested with Dr. Martin

---

1   For those not familiar with Rhode Island speak, a bubbler is a water fountain. Don't know where it came from, but it's what we call it!

Luther King Jr., Malcolm X, and other leaders. They marched together, holding signs letting people know about the unfairness of it all. Finally, after more and more people joined in the fight, after Miss Rosa Parks was arrested for refusing to give up her seat in the front of the bus, and after Dr. King spoke to a huge crowd of people in front of the Lincoln Memorial in Washington, D.C., Congress passed the Civil Rights Act of 1964, which said that you can't treat people differently because of their race, their religion, or whether they're a girl."

Mr. Goldberg summed it up. "Okay, so it sounds like it got pretty bad, and it took a lot of people joining together before big change happened. Sheila, can you tell us the story of the 19th Amendment?"

Sheila stepped in front of Byron and cleared her throat. "I'd be happy to. Let me tell you how it was in colonial times. Women were not even considered citizens back then. They couldn't choose the job they wanted. They couldn't own property. Heck, it was like they *were* property!"

Jessie sat up and leaned forward. "Really?" she asked aloud.

"Yeah, Jessie. For real. Like if you wanted to open up a fashion boutique for all your fancy clothes, your husband would have to buy it for you and then *allow* you to work there. No kidding."

"Well, what if I didn't get married?" Jessie asked. "What if I wanted to do things myself?"

"No can do, Sister," Sheila shook her head.

Mr. Goldberg asked, "So what did people do to try to change this situation, Sheila? Byron told us about protests. What happened with women's rights?"

"Same thing, Mr. G., same thing," Sheila said. "Women protested, made speeches and all that. One time, this awesome woman named Susan B. Anthony actually tried to vote. And she was taken away in handcuffs!" Sheila put her wrists together and held her hands to the sky. "When other women stood with signs in front of the White House, they got arrested for blocking traffic even though they were just standing on the sidewalk! Then some women even went on a hunger strike in jail, refusing to eat until they were let go. Finally, after like a hundred years of yelling about it, in 1920 women were allowed to vote when the 19th Amendment was passed."

"Okay," Mr. Goldberg said, "it looks like we have some common themes here. We've got large groups of citizens who don't have certain rights. And it sounded like there were a lot of people who, for whatever reason, didn't want this to change. Question is, why? Do you think they just wanted to stay with what was familiar, what was comfortable?"

We all wondered the same thing. Mr. Goldberg continued, "It took a long time and a lot of effort to make this kind of big change happen. People had to educate others around them about the need for change, and they needed to put pressure on those in power to make that change. So . . . did it work? Once these laws were passed, did things really change? Byron?"

"Well," said Byron, "it was slow. Really slow. And it was kind of a rough road. People got arrested. People got hurt. People got killed. I was just . . .just . . . kind of shocked when I did this report. I mean, my parents always told me about racism when they were growing up, but I didn't realize how unfair things were and how much it took to make things right."

Mr. Goldberg asked, "Sheila? Did things change once the 19th amendment was passed?"

"Same thing—not at first. Women did get the right to vote, and lots did in the very next election. But really, now that I've learned all this, I'm noticing that the people yapping at me in those political commercials around election time are almost all guys! And we haven't had a woman president yet!"

"Ah, but we can!" Mr. Goldberg said, his index finger poking up toward the ceiling. "We can! And that is the point here, right? That our country, our society, was humming along, with ideas like 'separate can be equal.' But then those rules got changed, and these changes were made by just everyday people, like you and I. And while change was slow, it happened."

Mr. Goldberg let us sit there, with this heavy blanket of new knowledge snuffing out any of the usual comments and jokes. Finally, he spoke. "Thank you Byron and Sheila. You've done a fantastic job. I think you deserve another round of applause, don't you think class?"

We all thought so too. We clapped some more for our classmates. Sheila pumped her fist into the air, and then knocked it with Byron's in a clenched symbol of brother- and sisterhood.

I raised my hand after Byron and Sheila sat down, because I had a really urgent question. "Mr. Goldberg," I said, "this is kind of like what happened to us just before Thanksgiving. We protested on the sidewalk in front of the school about how Greenwood needs to recycle more. And then Mr.

Musgrove came out and like . . . squashed it!" I slapped my hand on my desk to demonstrate.

"Really?" Mr. Goldberg asked and leaned forward in his chair, like Uncle James but without all that pride, just pure interest. "What did he say?"

Carlos spoke up. "He said we were disrupting dismissal. Now, I can see his point, but still, posters in the hall just won't make change happen."

"Yeah!" Sheila said loudly. "He was all like, get off my sidewalk! I was like, we have a right to free speech! Don't we, Mr. G?"

"Well," Mr. Goldberg stroked his beard in thought, "not really. Especially not when your speech is disrupting dismissal and making things unsafe for kids trying to get to their buses."

"But Mr. Musgrove basically said that we're not going to really do anything to help our planet." I said. "We're just supposed to hang up a bunch of posters and that's it? That's not what we're learning in here. It seems like it takes a lot more than that to create change."

There went Mr. Goldberg's smile again. "Arlene, you're right. It does take a lot more to create change." And there went Mr. Goldberg's index finger again, pointing at the ceiling, "However," and then he pointed at his head, "you've got to be smart!

You've got to use good judgment. Holding a protest on a crowded sidewalk at dismissal time, with buses pulling in and out is not a good idea. Maybe we should discuss what would be a good—"

And then the bell rang for lunch.

With a clap of his hands, Mr. Goldberg dismissed us to the cafeteria. "We'll talk more about this in the next social studies class," he called after us.

SLIPPERY SLOP

"*Dramatic*," I said.

"What did your uncle mean by that though?" Sheila asked. "How much more dramatic could we be than shouting out rhymes during dismissal and getting yelled at by the principal?"

While we munched on our lunch, we discussed the next steps in our action plan. Not the action plan we wrote with Mrs. Sweeney. As far as our gang was concerned, that thing should be thrown right into Greenwood's overflowing trash cans. That was a NO-action plan, meant to please people like Mr. Musgrove and make it look like we were doing something when we really weren't.

"I don't know," I told Sheila. "Uncle James didn't say what he meant by dramatic. And then the baby started crying, it got all busy—we never got to talk about it again on Thanksgiving."

"Look," Byron started to say something. But then he had to finish chewing. We all waited until, finally, he swallowed hard. "Look. We gotta do something. Make a move. Nothing is gonna happen if we don't. Did Martin Luther King just stand around and talk? Well, okay, yes he did, but his speeches were amazing, and he also did stuff. He went to jail! He marched on Washington!" Byron stood up and marched in place, staring upward at an imaginary Lincoln Memorial. "Rosa Parks walked to the front of the bus and sat down!" He plopped back down on the cafeteria bench with a thud. "We've got to do something, something big."

Sheila slapped her hand on the table. "I agree! Something huge!"

"We'll get in trouble though," Lauren warned. I didn't know why Lauren was even sitting here with us. I guess because Maddie was at our table, and now they're all BFFs. I felt our group was really growing closer with all we were doing with the recycling stuff, and Lauren and Maddie were just hanging out on the edge. No one would tell them to get lost, but they didn't feel a part of all this either.

"So?" Carlos added his logic. "So we get in trouble.

So did everyone else who took a stand for something. That's the way it is. Making change means taking risks."

Jessie leaned in. "You know what? I agree with you." She paused because she knew how surprising this news was to all of us. "Musgrove had some nerve. Nobody tells me where and when I can talk to people." Then she stared at Byron. "But! Let me just be clear: I am *not* going to juvie."

"You're not gonna go to juvie!" Joey snorted. "You'll go to detention, but so what? I'm there every day."

"Wait!" I said. "If we're going to do this, we need to think hard about it first. Everyone, think hard." I put my hands on the side of my head to power up my brain. They all did the same, even Lauren. "Now, close your eyes. Think. Understand. We may get in trouble. We may suffer. We may be tortured. But we may make Greenwood more green. We may help save Mother Earth!" I stretched my hands to the ceiling to call to Mother Earth herself. I imagined her smiling down on me, in this little cafeteria in the tiny state of Rhode Island. We had a moment together.

I opened my eyes and looked around. Everyone was staring at me like I had two heads.

Sheila laughed and slapped my back. "Good show, Arlene! Anyway, let's figure out what to do. What could be dramatic? What would get people's attention, especially Mr. Musgrove?"

Joey smiled his sneaky smile. He nodded slowly, to no one in particular. He was definitely thinking of a plan. "I know," he said. "I know just what we could do. Oh yeah, this is gonna be good."

We all bent our heads together to listen. And it was good, so good! We had to swear ourselves to ultimate secrecy.

We all sat back up, full to the brim with an amazing plan of action. Carlos announced in his serious, presidential tone, "We are about to embark on a treacherous journey. Join if you have the courage. Know that it carries great risks, but could mean great change. Place your hand in, to signal unity." And he stretched his hand into the center of our group.

Courage, did he say? That was my calling. I slapped my hand on Carlos's with a grin. Joey whacked his hand on ours, slamming them onto the table. Sheila came down on top, then Byron, and finally Jessie to top it all off. Slap, slap, slap.

Then we waited. We looked at Lauren. With a wrinkle in her forehead and a quick shake of her head, she left our table. Maddie followed.

The rest of us still had our hands together in the center of the table. Carlos put his other hand on top of the pile. "*Si se peude*." he said quietly. "It can be done."

We all had our assignments in order to carry out Joey's plan as soon as lunch was over. I walked straight to the art room instead of out the back door to the playground for recess. I snuck around corners like an international spy avoiding capture. Most classes were outside, but still, it was tricky to get all the way down that hallway completely undetected, especially in my leg braces. Finally, I got what I came for and headed back to our meeting point.

I was sweating again. Maybe I should start wearing deodorant. Chris did. He'd come out of his room smelling like a forest or something. Hopefully they had deodorant that smelled like something other than the woods, like maybe flowers. Or chocolate ice cream.

I turned the corner to the main hallway, dragging my package as quietly as I could. I saw Carlos and Byron coming out of the cafeteria, bringing their stuff too. And there was Jessie creeping out of the main office. Hers was the hardest assignment of all, but she could handle it. She walked around the school like she owned the place anyway, so marching into the main office to get something was like no big deal for her.

I stopped just outside the door to Mr. Musgrove's office. Carlos, Byron, and Jessie got there a few minutes later. Then Sheila appeared, pushing her bundle from the direction of the older kids' classrooms. The five of us waited for our leader. I noticed a handwritten sign on the staff bathroom across the hall from Mr. Musgrove's office, reading "Out of Order!" That was weird. Kids clogged up toilets all the time, but the grown-ups could usually keep their bathroom working.

Finally, down the hall a bit, the door to the boys' bathroom flew open, and Joey came racing out, hauling two trash cans behind him with one hand, paper towels flying in the air, his free hand waving wildly in our direction.

"Code red! Go! Go!" Joey screamed. "Get out! Code red, CODE RED!"

We froze for a few seconds, our brains trying to process Joey's frantic shouts. Then we saw the reason he was so panicked. The boys' bathroom door flew open again, and Mr. Musgrove came racing after Joey, his shirttail hanging out and toilet paper stuck to the bottom of his shoe. He was scrambling so hard to catch Joey that he slipped on the toilet paper and made a beautiful dive onto the floor, like he was sliding head first into home plate to score the winning run. For a second, a real split second, I wanted to yell "Safe!" and slice the air with my arms like a big-league umpire. Now that would've been *really* funny!

But this was no time for fun. We had a mission to complete. Joey reached us, shoving his two trash cans into the group with the eight others we brought from the cafeteria, the art room, classrooms and the copy machine in the main office. Then we threw open the door to Mr. Musgrove's office and turned all of them over, emptying their contents onto the floor, shouting "Save our planet!"

Our dramatic action left a huge pile of garbage on the floor in front of Mr. Musgrove's big desk. Tator Tots rolled down ramps of construction paper, and purple paint oozed across the green tile floor. Wet paper towels were stuck like spitballs onto cardboard pieces, which were glued with applesauce to Styrofoam trays. It was like a shaggy carpet of garbage covering the entire area between Musgrove's desk and the door. To us, this mound of slop was a symbol of how we would eventually destroy our planet if we didn't make a change right now. We stood back to view our mission accomplished, but just for a moment. And then off we ran out of the school.

Dramatic, yes.

REWIND NOT AVAILABLE

Um, yeah, "dramatic" wasn't really the right word. "Horribly wrong," perhaps? "Enormous, unforgiveable mistake" might work. "Something we'll regret for the rest of our lives?" Yes, that might be a more appropriate way to look at it.

To say the very, very least, we were in very, very big trouble. I thought last year's boy-girl war was bad. That was a six-horse merry-go-round compared to this life-threatening roller coaster we had boarded, a high-speed plunge to the ground with no seat belt.

I tried to think about Dr. King, Cesar Chavez, Susan B. Anthony, and Rosa Parks. Did they feel like me? Were they desperately trying to find the rewind button? After their big protests, were they more scared than they'd ever been before?

Of course we were called back into the school from recess within minutes of our escape. Mr. Musgrove knew exactly who was to blame, and we knew that owning up to your social action was part of the deal. Rosa Parks did not wear a mask. If you believe in what you're doing, there's no sense in doing it anonymously.

By five o'clock in the afternoon after our big protest, we were knee-deep in smelly food, cleaning up the cardboard scraps, wet paper towels, and all things strange and disgusting that get thrown into school trash cans. We had on rubber gloves, but they didn't keep me from wanting to throw up. I couldn't tell if my nausea was from handling all this garbage or from my guilt over what we had just done.

Finally, Mr. Peterson came by with his yellow bucket of soapy water and stringy mop. He shook his head at us. "You kids really did it this time. Shame. Just a shame." And he looked right at me. "What were you thinking?"

We answered with teary silence.

"Go on, get outta here. Your parents'll be here soon." Then he called out, "Mr. Musgrove! The kids are about done."

Mr. Musgrove stomped down the hallway. I swear I saw steam coming off his bald head. He stopped in front of us, crossed his arms and stared down hard. "Line up by the front door and wait for your parents. I've talked to all of them, and I would expect that you'll have further consequences at home. But tomorrow you'll also begin serving your consequences here: you'll clean the cafeteria during recess for the next month, and before you leave every day you'll help Mr. Peterson collect the trash from each room in this school. And Carlos, you've demonstrated today that you no longer possess the qualities necessary to be leader of the SGA. The vice president will take over, and you're banned for the rest of the year."

We all gasped at this news. But Carlos's face never changed. He stared right back at Mr. Musgrove and nodded.

As Mr. Musgrove turned back toward his office, we all shuffled slowly to the front door.

"Carlos, I'm so sorry," I said.

"Yeah, jeez, Carlos," Byron added. "That's horrible. It's like you were impeached!"

Joey reached ahead of him to rest his hand on Carlos's shoulder. "Tough break, buddy. That stinker Musgrove!"

Carlos stopped and turned toward us. "Guys—" he looked quickly at Sheila, "I mean, everyone . . .

it's fine. We all went into this with our eyes open. I accept my consequences. And anyways, it's not over. Far from it."

We all stared at him. Was he kidding? It was over for me! *Way* over!

"No talking!" Mr. Musgrove shouted at us from his doorway. "You are to wait silently for your parents. One more word and there'll be additional consequences for all of you!"

My shirt was drenched with sweat under my winter coat as I waited for my parents to pick me up. I would need some sort of super-strength deodorant if this little adventure wasn't over.

When I saw our red van pull into the parking lot, some invisible force grabbed my stomach and twisted it into a triple knot. I would have swallowed hard but my mouth was as dry as little cracked ovals of watercolor paints. My hands were shaking as I picked up my backpack. The group watched me like a soldier marching off to a battle, one from which I might never return. I nodded at my partners in crime, and they nodded solemnly back. The cold air felt good on my face as I stepped outside and headed to my doom.

For the first time, I was thrilled that there were no middle seats in the van. I sat way in back, with lots of space between me and my parents. They were silent as I buckled in, as I figured they would be. They probably wouldn't speak until we got home. But if I had to wait that long for my world to cave in, I thought my nervousness would strangle me.

"Mom, Dad, listen, I—"

"Do *not*. Say. A word." Mom said, her voice cold and sharp like icicles.

I blinked back tears and looked out the window. I really wanted to talk to Uncle James right then. He would make me feel better about what we did. He would understand why we decided to take a stand. Maybe he would even agree with what we did.

Well . . . maybe not.

When we pulled into the garage, Mom backed her wheelchair out with force, slammed it into forward motion, and flew down the van ramp then up the ramp into our house. I shuffled behind her, with Dad stone-faced and last in line. We filed into the kitchen. I wasn't sure what I was supposed to do. I put my backpack down in its spot under the counter and sat down at the kitchen table, waiting for my punishment like a prisoner before a firing squad.

Mom rolled toward me, stopped, opened her mouth, and then closed it again. Finally she said,

"I can't even talk to you right now," and sped away down the hall to her bedroom.

Dad shook his head. "Arlene, I don't know what to say either. I mean, really, I can't begin to imagine what got into you. Did you think this through at all? Did you stop and think what the consequences would be?"

That was what was so weird about this whole situation. We actually did think, with hands on our heads and eyes closed, we did think this whole thing through. We knew what the risks were. And we did it anyway.

Mom flew back into the kitchen and screeched to a stop across from me at the table. "What were you thinking?" she demanded.

"That's what Dad just asked me," I said quietly.

Like that firing squad I was waiting for, she peppered me with shouted words. "I don't care if Dad just asked you that, I'm asking you that right now. I am so incredibly disappointed in you for your poor judgment, your irresponsibility, and your awful behavior. You will not see the light of day until you're sixteen, do you hear me?"

As ridiculous as that last sentence was, I knew enough to simply agree with Mom. "Yes," I whispered.

"Here's what's going to happen: You'll do your

homework. You'll eat your dinner. You'll go to bed. You'll get up, go to school, and *repeat*!" She whipped her wheelchair around and whizzed back down the hall. "Until you're sixteen!" she called over her shoulder.

I sighed heavily. I always feel a little better after I get grounded. The pain feels good, feels right. It shrinks my guilt, just a little. While I believed in what we did, why we did it, I hated that I disappointed my parents. It was such a high price for saving the planet.

Dad began to get dinner started, boiling water for pasta and taking out a package of beef for meatballs. At least we were having something good to eat. I would have to be thankful for the little things from now on—until I turned sixteen.

After dinner I brushed my teeth to get ready for bed. It was seven o'clock, my bedtime when I was five years old and now again when I was ten. Oh, well. I deserved it.

Chris came into the bathroom to grab his toothbrush too. "I got a study group meeting tonight. Katie will be there, and I gotta smell *fresh*!" He bent down to breathe into my face. He hadn't brushed his teeth yet, and I fell backwards, nearly melting from the stink.

I spoke through two hands covering my nose and mouth. "Oh my gosh, Chris, you're going to need disinfectant for that!"

He smiled, closed his eyes, and began to brush. He loved torturing me, always had. He spit a mouthful of foam into the sink and leaned over, continuing to brush his teeth. His big, teenage body covered practically the whole counter. It looked like I was going to have to wait til he was done to brush my own teeth. Well, at least that would give me a few more minutes before I had to go to bed.

Chris spat again, rinsed, and then spat that out with a big pwah! Then he leaned with one elbow on the sink and looked right into my eyes. "I feel for ya, Squirt. You're in deep doo-doo."

"Nooo kidding," I said, rolling my eyes.

"But I gotta say, it's pretty impressive. Dumping trash in the principal's office—not too shabby."

I shrugged. His admiration didn't mix well with all of my guilt and regret. It felt weird.

Then he put his forehead against mine. Talk about weird. "It's gonna be tough for you for a while with Mom and Dad. Hang in there, Sis. I got your back."

He stood up, shot his toothbrush under the water

for a second, threw it on the counter, and clomped out of the bathroom.

Good ol' Chris.

Keeps me on my toes, that brother.

SAVING UNCLE JAMES

As we waited on the cafeteria floor the next morning for the first bell to ring, Joey was declared the
winner of the Worst Punishment Ever Contest.
Not only was he on total lockdown like the rest
of us, but he had to clean both bathrooms in his
house, do the dishes every night, and walk his dog
every afternoon, *including picking up the poop*. Apparently his parents felt that the right punishment
for dumping garbage should involve grime, crusty
food, and poop.

Lauren came into the cafeteria and sat down near
me, but not really next to me. I could feel her looking at me, but I didn't turn toward her. In my head
I pictured her standing on the opposite side of a

Grand Canyon–size crack. I could barely see the speck of her.

"Hi Arlene," she said.

I couldn't find my voice. Someone had stolen it right from my throat.

"You okay?" she asked. "I mean, after what happened yesterday?"

I shrugged. Maybe I needed to put out an all-points-bulletin on my voice box: LOST! One smart-alecky voice. Huge reward. If found, do not use. Will result in big trouble.

"Did you get in a lot of trouble?" she asked.

"Yeah." Ah. There you are!

"What happens now with our recycling project?"

"I dunno. Whatever. Maybe we can just put up the posters again and wait around for a miracle to happen."

"Arlene," Lauren said. "It's still a good cause!"

"Yeah, well, you'd better face it. Nothing's going to happen. You could wallpaper this whole school with posters, but nothing's going to change. At least the rest of us tried to actually do something."

"Yeah and look where it got you! Absolutely

nowhere. Now Mr. Musgrove is so angry he'll never listen to us."

"Newsflash: he wasn't listening to us anyway."

"You don't know that," Lauren said quietly.

She sat there, studying the faded gray and white squares of the cafeteria floor. I sat there, studying the unraveling shoelace on my left sneaker. Kids chattered all around us, but in between Lauren and me, it was just all muffled, and stuffy, and, really, just kind of yucky.

I sighed and rested my chin on my hands, my elbows on my knees. The bell rang, signaling us all to go to class. I turned to the side and put my hands flat on the floor. I pushed up to get on my feet, but today, I really had trouble. A few weeks ago, Ms. Farley had suggested that we leave a small chair in the cafeteria for me to sit in while we wait for the bell to ring. She thought it was too difficult for me to get up from the floor without help.

Personally, I thought she should take that baby chair and sit her own behind in it, perhaps in another school far, far away.

I suffered two days of silence from Mom before she finally talked to me. I mean, she talked to me when necessary, but she didn't really *talk* to me until Friday evening, a couple of days after our Garbage Dump Protest.

I was getting into bed. It was 7:15 pm. OMG!

Mom appeared in my doorway and spoke to me from there, probably staying far away from me to remind me that she was still very upset, even though she was finally talking to me. "Arlene," she said, "you've got to help me out here. I doubt I will understand, but try to explain what you were thinking when you decided to dump mounds of garbage in your principal's office."

I pulled the covers up to my chin and looked at Mom from behind my comforter shield. "I just thought . . . I felt like—" Ah! How could I explain this? Then an idea popped into my brain. "I felt like it was time to create a ruckus."

Mom went full throttle toward my bed. I ducked under my covers quickly to protect myself. I lowered them just a teeny bit when I heard the whir of her wheelchair stop.

"Ruckus?" she demanded. "What do you mean by ruckus?"

"Um, I was just saying that I thought . . . we all thought . . . I mean, we all felt like nothing was ever going to change. Mr. Musgrove said there's no money in the budget to do anything different about recycling, and posters on a wall don't do anything. We needed to take action. That's what we're learning about in social studies, that when you need big changes you have to take big action. And Uncle James said we should do something dramatic."

Mom leaned closer to my face. "Uncle James said what?"

Oh, shoot, now Uncle James was going to be in trouble. I wished I could snatch the words "Uncle James" out of the air and shove them back into my mouth.

"Um, well, Uncle James and I were talking about how our rally on the sidewalk didn't really change anything, and so—"

"What rally on the sidewalk?" Mom shouted.

Oh, right. Mom didn't know about that. Shoot. Man, was I in deep! "Well, it wasn't really a rally. We just made up some rhymes about how we should all recycle more, and we told the rhymes to our friends." I watched her face carefully for an anger explosion. It looked safe so far, so I took another step. "You know, like, at dismissal time."

"So you marched along the sidewalk yelling about recycling while everyone was trying to get on the buses and go home? Wasn't that a bit disruptive?"

"Yeah, that's what Mr. Musgrove said. But we thought we had the right to free speech."

Mom turned her head to the side and mumbled, "Right to free speech—" like she was talking to some invisible person standing next to her who was as shocked as she was at this idea of free speech. She sighed and turned back to me. She looked more tired than angry at this point. "Oo-kaayy. Arlene, what made you think you had a right to free speech?" Mom tilted her head back and forth at the words "right to free speech." I knew that if she could, she would have done air quotes around those words, but the head wiggle said it all. She didn't buy this whole free speech thing.

"Um . . . that's what Uncle James always says." Darn! Poor Uncle James!

Tap, tap, tap went the finger on Mom's right hand, letting me know her anger level was about to reach its boiling point.

She shook her head, like she needed a moment to process all the information she had just received. "Go to bed," was all she said.

"'Night!" I called. A cold silence answered.

What a mess!

As soon as the sounds of her wheelchair got soft

enough to mean she was in the kitchen, I jumped out of bed. And of course fell flat on my face.

"Arlene!" Dad called from the kitchen. "You okay?"

"Yeesss!" I yelled. I waited a minute to be sure they weren't coming down to my room and also to allow the pain to go away just a little. Then I crawled to Chris's room, really going back in time to when I was a toddler, both with my bedtime and my mode of transportation. Truly, it was the safest way to travel to Chris's room since I had no braces on, and I needed to go quietly, no more falling.

I knelt at the end of Chris's bed, which unfortunately put me square in front of his smelly feet. I wondered if he was going to shower or what? I guess he had plenty of time to do that because the sun had practically just gone down.

I peeked above the end of his bed. He had his earbuds in his ears, of course, and was supposedly doing his homework, reading some humongous book. I would have tickled his feet to get his attention, but I didn't want to touch them. I crawled around to the side of the bed and peeked over again.

His eyes were closed! How does he get such good grades by sleeping through his homework?

I rested my elbows on the side of his bed and

punched him lightly on his shoulder. His eyes opened slowly, and he looked over. It was like a sleeping dragon awakening, slow at first but then totally shaky like an earthquake. He rolled his head one way, stretched, threw his arm out the other way to stretch that, almost whacking me in the eye. I ducked, but then he threw his covers to the side, sending me back down to avoid being smothered by his comforter. Finally, he seemed about done, and I pushed my hair off my face, reached up, and raised my head over the side of his bed again.

Chris finally noticed me. "Squirt. Whaddya want? Aren't you supposed to be in bed, you little prisoner?"

"Shhh!" I whispered fiercely. "Quiet! Mom and Dad can't know I'm in here! Listen, I need to use your phone."

"What? Why? No. I don't have a lot of minutes left."

"Please, Chris! Please. I gotta talk to Uncle James. He's the one who said I should dump garbage in Mr. Musgrove's office, and now Mom knows that, and she's going to kill him!"

Chris laughed. I didn't see what was funny.

"Uncle James said to dump garbage in your

principal's office?" Chris asked with a doubtful raise of his eyebrows.

"Well, okay, no, not exactly, but whatever, we had this talk at Thanksgiving, and he kind of said we should do something dramatic, so I was trying to explain to Mom where I got the idea from, so I said Uncle James, and now Mom is definitely going to freak out at him, so please, please, Chris! Let me use your phone to talk to Uncle James! This whole thing just keeps getting worse and worse, and I'm going to get him in so much trouble, and everything is such a mess. I'm ruining everything."

I could feel the tears. They were on their way. I swallowed, trying to push them back down. I swallowed again. Nope, not working. I blinked, I swallowed, and I clenched my teeth together. The tears were all bubbled up in my eyeballs, but they hadn't spilled over yet. Maybe I could do it . . . nope, whoosh, down they came, splish splash, all onto Chris's comforter. I bent my head down, just to catch all this blubbering on my arms instead of soaking Chris's bed. My mind jumped from one icky thing to another: the sloppy garbage, my parents' disappointment, how awful things were with Lauren. They were all making me feel sick. I felt my brother's big hand on my hair.

"Arlene. Come on, it's gonna be okay. Hang in there. Here, use my phone. Save Uncle James. That's one less person in trouble over this." He bent his head down to try to look into my eyes. They were too blubbery, and I didn't want to look at him, but I did anyway. My big brother. He really did have my back.

He smiled at me. "It's really going to be okay."

I nodded because, obviously, I couldn't speak. He handed me his phone, and I tried to dial, but it was like trying to read underwater with all these tears in my eyes. Chris dialed Uncle James and handed me the phone.

I sniffled and put the phone to my ear. Chris handed me a tissue, and I tried to mop up my face a little bit.

"Hello," Uncle James said. "Chris? What's up, man?"

I sniffled again. My voice sounded like it was coming from underwater too. "Uncle James, it's not Chris. It's me, Arlene."

"Arlene! What's wrong? Are you okay?"

"Yeah," I said weakly. "Well, no. Not at all okay. But I'm not hurt or anything. I'm just in a lot of trouble."

Uncle James spoke quickly. "Whoa, what kind of

trouble? Where are you? I'll come get you. What's going on?"

"No, no, I'm not, like, *in* trouble, in jail or something. I'm grounded and stuff. It's kind of *like* jail, I suppose, but I haven't been arrested or anything."

"Arlene! Tell me what's going on? I'm freaking out over here."

I sighed. I told him the whole story. Uncle James listened to every word.

"Oh man, my little Curly Whirly. You are in deep."

"Um, I think you're in deep too."

"Hey. Don't you worry about me! Your mom doesn't scare me." He paused. "Well, okay, she does a little. But that's just because she's like a fierce mother lion around you cubs. She will protect you no matter what. But no worries. I'll talk to her. I'll man up. I told you to get dramatic, I did. That's on me."

"But Uncle James, I know you didn't tell me to dump garbage and all that, but still, we had to do *something* didn't we? I mean, Mr. Musgrove won't do anything if all we do is put up a bunch of posters, or even do a little rally at dismissal. He just shoos us away, like we're annoying little flies. Were we totally wrong?"

"No, no, not totally. But yeah, kind of . . . um . . . pretty much wrong, yeah. I mean, you need to do something dramatic, but you can't do something that's so against the rules, and you can't do something that targets one person like that, even Mr. Muskrat. That's why Dr. King was so good at this. He was like, hey, we're just walking, just talking, just marching along this public street here. We're just standing around here in front of the Lincoln Memorial. Oh, there's a quarter of a million of us? Hmm, what does that tell you, Mr. President?"

I laughed at the thought of the great Dr. King talking like Uncle James. The smile felt good on my face.

Suddenly, Uncle James blurted out, "Oh, I have it! You know, some of the great revolutionaries have used protest theater to make their point and get support for big change. Maybe you could do something like that? Do you guys do school plays there?"

"Protest theater? You mean like, do a play about why we need to recycle?"

"Exactly! Make it really powerful, but unlike your protest on the sidewalk, it's perfectly legit! You're just putting on a school play. Who can have a problem with that?"

"We do have a school play, but it's usually like *Peter Pan* or something. Not something with a message. And Mrs. Chesterfield runs the drama program. I don't think she'd really be up for doing protest theater."

"Well, I hate to say this, but you may have to step outside the process."

"I have no idea what that means."

"I mean, you'll have to do it on your own, like you're doing with this whole recycling action plan. Organize it yourselves. Do it on a Saturday, at a playground or something. Let everyone know about it yourselves, spread the word through social media."

"Uncle James. I'm ten. We're not allowed to use social media yet."

"Ah, well, okay, whatever, I'm sure you can figure out how to spread the word. The point is, you do this outside of the school day, but you still reach everybody. It'll be a fun community event with a powerful message."

I could hear Uncle James getting excited. Oh no, this was how I ended up in all this trouble!

But still, I couldn't help but ride this wave with Uncle James. He was like the Pied Piper, and I was just one of the little kids trailing after him.

"I don't know. I'll have to think about that, maybe talk to the other kids."

Uncle James hit the brakes just then. He could hear the hesitation in my voice, and it was like he remembered again why we were talking on the phone. "You know, Arlene, no pressure. I mean, I understand if you want to just lie low, give this up for now. You've been through a lot."

I sighed. "Thanks, Uncle James. Thanks for talking with me, for listening. You gonna be okay? Mom's going to call you, you know."

"Hey, Arlene My Queen, I got that covered. Get some sleep tonight. Let all this rest a while."

"G'night. Love you."

"Love you, too. Talk to ya soon."

I handed the phone back to Chris. "What did he say?" Chris asked.

"A lot. A lot of stuff. I gotta go think."

"Yeah, but are you okay?"

My brain felt like it was going to be crushed under the weight of all that I was thinking about. "I don't know what I am. But hopefully I'll figure it out eventually. Thanks for your phone. I'll pay you for the minutes."

"Nah, don't worry about it." Chris put his earbuds back in his ears, and our brotherly-sisterly moment was over.

I crawled back to my room and up into my bed.

Of course I couldn't sleep. My head actually hurt. I kept hearing Uncle James's voice, deep and slow like some DJ had added special effects to it, making it a booming, thunderous announcement: "Give this up . . . lie low . . . let things rest a while."

These words were like acid burning a hole in that gut of mine. I just can't do that; it's just not me.

Let's go, then. Round three.

STEP-BY-STEP

My friends all liked the idea of holding a protest theater play, although not everyone really understood what I was talking about. Frankly, I wasn't completely sure either, but I figured once we started writing the script it would flow. Even Lauren seemed to go along with this idea, although I hadn't planned on including her. She just kind of listened in when I was telling the others. But maybe if she joined us in this, things could go back to normal. My mouth smiled at this thought without me even telling it to.

Now, it wasn't like we could just perform a play in the middle of school. No, this thing had to be carefully planned out. And we certainly weren't going to rely on Joey to do the planning. Look what happened last time! Luckily, planning is my thing.

Step One. On my way from the cafeteria to my classroom that morning, I figured I'd find Mrs. Landers somewhere. As president of the PTA this year, she was at school practically every day, looking very, very busy. It seemed like she worked as hard as the teachers.

Sure enough, there she was stapling flyers and things to a bulletin board in the hallway.

"Um, excuse me, Mrs. Landers," I said, pulling my Polite Voice out of my handy voice toolkit. "I was wondering if I could ask you a favor?"

Mrs. Landers bent down all over me. "Well of course, Sweetie. What is it?"

Like a little kid, I opened my arms and waved my hands as I talked. Something about the way Mrs. Landers leaned over me and spoke to me in that gooey voice just made me feel like a preschooler. "So, yeah, as part of social studies we're going to put on a little show Friday after school about why we need to be nice to the environment and all that. Mr. Goldberg asked me to ask you if you could get the word out to parents about our little show-thing." I opened my eyes wide, then blinked purposefully, like a sweet little cartoon kitten.

Mrs. Landers put her hand on my cheek. "Oh, sure, Honey! Anything for Mr. Goldberg! What a wonderful thing you're doing! I'd be happy to make up a flyer for the bulletin board here and—"

"No, no! No flyer on a bulletin board. No, because, well, actually it's a surprise for Mr. Musgrove. A surprise . . . yes, to show him what great things the fifth grade can do!" (If Mrs. Landers only knew what *disruptive* things we could do!)

"Oh, well, then maybe I could put something on the parent email listserv? Almost all families have signed up to participate, but teachers and principals aren't on it." She bent down even further over me and whispered, "Would that work to keep our little secret?"

I whispered back, "Ooh, great idea, yes! Thanks Mrs. Landers! You're the best!"

"And you are just a wonderful inspiration to us all!"

Huh? Inspiration? Whatever. We got on the listserv.

Suh-weet! Step One—complete! On to Step Two . . . ummm . . . it's got to come through! (Sorry, sometimes I just have to rhyme.)

Later that day, I shoved my lunch into my mouth, and then immediately asked to use the bathroom. It was 12:18 p.m., and I stood all nervous by the main office for Mr. Musgrove to march down this hall toward his office, sometime between 12:15 and 12:20. I knew he does this every day because any good planner does her research. Joey called this research "getting intel." Whatever, I knew that Mr. Musgrove checks in at the cafeteria every day in the middle of lunch and then strides down the hall to his office where I was guessing he chows down on his own lunch. But who knows? Do principals even eat? Burp? Sleep? Pee? (Eww!)

And sure enough, there he was. His military stomps got weaker when he saw me waiting, like he was afraid of what new trouble I'd brought. I tried to head him off.

"Mr. Musgrove! Hi!" I chirped.

He stopped in front of me and looked down. "Yes, Arlene? Hi. What're you doing?"

"Oh? Me?" I put a hand to my chest. "Well, I just wanted to really quickly let you know that the PTA is doing their regular Playground Clean-up Day this Friday after school, and the recycling team is helping, you know, because that helps the environment and everything. Mrs. Landers asked me to let you know."

He stared down at me some more. "Okay." Stare, stare, stare. "Thanks."

"Okay." I felt kind of frozen. "So, um, yeah.

That'll do it." I turned to walk toward the door to the playground. "Thanks," I called.

"Oh, Arlene." Mr. Musgrove held his hand up to me. "Wait a minute."

Uh-oh. He was on to me.

"Clean it up really well. Got that? You kids still owe me for the mess you made."

"Oh, yes, yes, absolutely. You're right, so right." I shouldn't have, but I kept talking. "Wait til you come in here on Monday, you won't even recognize the playground. You'll say, wow! Who took away our old playground and replaced it with this crazy clean playground. You'll wonder what amazing little elves stopped by to clean—"

"Arlene!" Mr. Musgrove snapped.

"Yes?"

"Enough."

"Right."

And I got out of there fast.

Weird how I'm the same "me" all day, but Mrs. Landers sees an "inspiration" and Mr. Musgrove sees a troublemaker.

I can't decide which one I like better.

TURTLE TRAP, PART 2

I was ready to handle anything with Mr. Musgrove. I was not ready for what happened with Lauren. But of course, the universe doesn't seem to ever listen to how I want my life to go. For some reason, the universe just seems to move me along whatever path it wants to, at whatever speed. And I just have to deal with it.

It was bad. I mean, like, worse than the worst, most awful, horrific, devastating, wish-the-earth-would-suck-you-down-into-its-fiery-core-where-you-will-burn-into-dismal-gray-ashes terrible. I'm afraid to even tell about it. But Mom says even awful, awful things can be important. You've got to face them. So here goes.

The last class of the day was art. We always

brought our backpacks and jackets to art, because Mrs. Armonte, our art teacher, liked to dismiss us right from there. She liked to fully use her "allotted creative time," she'd say.

Art was usually totally fun. Mrs. Armonte was like a burst of cold breeze from an air conditioner on a sticky summer day, the kind of thing that makes you go, "Ahhh." She was just completely refreshing. Her hair was thick, curly, and clearly not interested in following directions. Actually, I doubted she ever tried to tame it. She would just shove it off her face with a paint-splattered hand, streaking her forehead with a bit of purple or green, and she really never seemed to care. Her usual outfit was overalls, tan workboots, and sweatshirts with the sleeves rolled way up so they didn't get in the way of her art. And she stared intently into your eyes whenever she talked to you, like she was trying to pull the art out of your soul. The great thing about her is that whatever idea you had for whatever project we were working on, she would always "LOVE IT!"

So I was psyched about our current project: a collage. Mrs. Armonte provided us with every material under the sun, and large containers of the stickiest glue ever made in order to paste this stuff to thick pieces of paper. Our only direction was to

"CREATE!" There were scraps of paper, of course, but also glitter, felt, buttons, pebbles, googly eyes, yarn, paper clips, tons of little white circles from a hole puncher, sand, the little rings that you rip off when you open a gallon of milk, shoelaces, even the little pointy plastic collar things from Mr. Armonte's business shirts. You name it, we had it. Looking over all this stuff, it occurred to me that Mrs. Armonte would have been a great spokesperson for our recycling campaign!

I had my collage all planned out. I wanted to feature pictures of horses, computers, and cellphones, just because I found some cool ones on the overflowing table of materials we could use, and I love horses. When Mrs. Armonte checked on my progress, she freaked and thought I was making a "brilliant statement on the connectedness of our society, from the Pony Express to Cyberspace." I just liked the pictures.

The thing is, I wanted the pictures to pop off the page. So I wanted them outlined in fluorescent colors, then framed with yarn, and glitter around the outside of that. I tried cutting the thin frames of fluorescent paper, but I couldn't get my fingers to work the scissors right. And the yarn was getting all gunked up with the glue, because again, my fingers are just too stiff. I looked around at everyone else speeding through their projects, and I could feel the frustration heating up my head.

Mrs. Armonte walked by and of course noticed this, because she examined my face as she talked to me and with her X-ray eyes could probably actually see the frustration burning my brain. "Arlene, here, let me get you some help for this while I finish checking everyone else's work." She held my paper up at her eye level with stretched out arms. She nodded her approval, put it back down on the table and snapped her fingers. "Lauren! You're almost done; you can help your friend cut these strips of paper and glue this yarn and then get back to your own project."

Lauren and I looked at each other. I suddenly felt very sad. Lauren helping me used to be the most comfortable thing in the world. But now we were in such an uncomfortable place.

Lauren sighed and scraped her chair along the floor until she was next to me. I told her quietly, "I need these colors cut thin, so it's just like a shadow, not a thick frame."

Lauren started cutting, but she was going too quickly. The strips were thin in some places and thick in others. "No, Lauren, can you do it all the same thickness?"

"Well, can't you just do one color? It'll be faster." Then she added, "Does the color really matter?"

Whoa! I blinked at this girl. She felt like a stranger. I stared past Lauren's head, out the window at spiky tree branches poking the gray sky. "It matters," I whispered.

She didn't answer. We worked in silence for a while, me struggling to cut some strips, and Lauren zipping through strips like she didn't even care how they looked. Then she hurriedly plopped a glob of glue on my paper and stuck a pile of yarn to it.

I squinted my eyes at my fingers again, trying to make them do what I needed them to do. I couldn't even watch Lauren anymore. Maybe I could just get this done myself. But my strips were still all crooked, all messed up and just ridiculous. I could feel tears bubbling up. No, not again! Get out of here!

"Here." Lauren handed me a bunch of strips and pushed my collage back at me. It was not at all what I hoped it would look like. Lauren slid her chair back to her spot and went back to work on her project. She was running out of time too, because Mrs. Armonte had made her help me.

I looked down at my collage. I wouldn't have time to get this right. Mrs. Armonte had said that this was the last week we were working on our collages because we had to move on to the next unit. I had placed my pictures so perfectly. It was a shame that the frames and glitter wouldn't be put on right. And the yarn. What about the yarn? It would have been so awesome!

I looked over at Lauren, chatting with Maddie next to her while she finished up her collage. There were little patches of sand that kind of looked like a beach scene, with bits of wood, Popsicle sticks, cottony clouds, yellow glitter sunshine. It was . . . awesome. Like mine should have been.

Should I ask her for more help? It was the last thing I wanted to do.

"Lauren?" I called. "Can you do this over again? It's not right. The strips are all different sizes, and the yarn is a mess."

Lauren looked up at the clock, looked over at my project, and then down at her own. She blinked her eyes quickly, bit her lip, and seemed to be thinking really hard about my question. She was stalling! Finally, she spoke, but like in a whisper. "Arlene, I just can't help you anymore." She stared down at her paper for a long minute. Then she looked up at me. Yep, she was crying. I couldn't tell if she was talking about helping me with this collage or helping me forever. I didn't really want to know the answer though. It was all I could do to hold in my tears too.

Mrs. Armonte called out, "You guys have just a few minutes left. Finish up, okay?" She walked by my table. "Arlene, do you need more help? Lauren, I thought you were going to cut these . . . " Mrs. Armonte looked up just then, as someone walked by the classroom.

Oh no. Oh no! NO!

"Ah! Great! Ms. Farley?" Mrs. Armonte called. "Ms. Farley? Come on in here a minute. Listen, can you help Arlene with this cutting? Just for a sec, just so she can finish up before the bell rings. I've got to get everyone else organized and cleaned up."

"Sure, I'd be happy to," Ms. Farley said as she approached me, ponytail bobbing as if it wasn't the worst moment of my life.

I lost the battle with my tears.

I couldn't do this. I heaved my backpack onto my shoulders, grabbed my jacket, and ran to get out of that room as fast as possible. Except I can't really run anymore. And so bam! Down I went, right in the aisle between two art tables. Just like Mom and I laughed about a few weeks back, which seemed like a lifetime ago, I fell, all twisted around, right over onto my big, heavy backpack, which slapped me down to the floor like a leash snaps back a little puppy trying to chase a passing squirrel. And, of course, I was stuck there. On the floor. A big, upside-down turtle.

Oh, earthly force that sucks people down into your fiery core and burns them to dismal gray ash: where are you now? Rescue me from this!

I opened my eyes, looked up, and saw like a million hands hovering in the air above my head, wanting to help me up. I saw Mrs. Armonte's, Byron's, Sheila's, Lauren's, Ms. Farley's. I shut my eyes, swiped one arm across my wet face, and swiped the other at the outstretched hands, like I was swatting at killer bees. I felt a little bad about that afterward. I knew they were only trying to help. But I was really in a bad place at that point, to say the least.

"NO!" I screamed. "I can do it myself!" Everyone backed away from me at that point, like I had frightened them. I knew they had never seen me like this, never seen me without my smile, my "positive outlook," as I had heard so many adults say about me. They had never seen that I get so frustrated sometimes I need to scream loud enough to make my lungs burn. They had never seen that sometimes I feel so angry I want to punch the wall until my knuckles bleed. They had never seen that sometimes, I'm just plain ol' sick of being the hero, the inspiration, Arlene the Courageous. They just didn't know that sometimes, I'm not such a hero. Sometimes I'm just an ordinary crankpot.

I tried to roll to one side, then the other. Didn't work. The bell rang. Oh great. Kids thankfully filed out the back door of the art room so they didn't have to trample over me. Mrs. Armonte and Ms. Farley kept trying to help me get up, but I ignored them completely.

"Look," a girl's voice said firmly. "Just leave her alone for a second, will you?"

I opened my eyes, which had been shut to help me ignore everyone. I saw boots next to my head—awesome-looking designer boots. My eyes traveled up, following the familiar leggings that fit perfectly, topped with a beautiful shirt that hung all stylish over the pants. Yes, I knew these clothes. Yes, I knew this person. I just couldn't for the life of me figure out why she was standing next to me, why she was standing up for me.

"You want me to help you up, or you want to do

it yourself?" Jessie asked, like she didn't really care either way.

"Help," I said simply.

"Here," she said. "Wiggle out of your backpack. It'll be easier to get up." And she held my backpack down as I scooted out of it. Silently, she held out her hand and pulled me up with strength I had no idea she had. She probably could beat Ms. Farley in an arm-wrestling contest I'd bet.

And then, Jessie and I walked out of the classroom together.

Jessie ended the silence as we walked to the buses. "You need to just let her go."

I, on the other hand, continued the silence.

"I've seen this before," Jessie went on. "Some people just can't handle things like CMT. Best thing is to just let them float on."

I took another moment of silence. Finally, I spoke: "Well, I think I can handle my own friendships, thanks anyway."

Jessie gave me her classic shrug. "Sure, fine."

Step, step, silent step. And then she did it again. "You should pick friends who know that you need help sometimes, but who also don't treat you like you're helpless."

I felt myself breathing fast. I hated getting friendship advice from Jessie, and I hated that it actually made sense. Before I could stop myself, I answered Jessie straight from my heart. "I thought Lauren was that person."

There went that shrug again, and she pulled a hairband out of her hair. "Apparently not. Doesn't make her a bad person, just someone who doesn't always get it. Or someone who used to get it but is now distracted by, like, her art project, or Maddie, or all that ice skating stuff they do."

I stared at this blond genius. *She* clearly got it. So why weren't we best friends?

I answered myself: she was just way too harsh. Smart, but harsh.

INDEPENDENT MAN

I sat alone on the bus. *Turtle floppers should sit alone,* I thought. And all the kids seemed to understand this. It was like we were all big magnets, and I was a south pole to their north. Anyone who came close to me was repelled by the force of my loserness.

Jessie did walk with me to the buses, that was true. And we talked a little more. Turns out, she's got an older brother too, but he's not like Chris. Jessie's brother, Robert, has to deal with stuff too, just like me, and so that must be why Jessie understood. Robert—not Bob, not Rob, not Bobby, he wants to be called *Robert*—has autism. Jessie said his mind is amazing. He thinks of things we would never realize in a million years. But his mind works so differently that other kids sometimes think he's weird.

ARLENE, THE REBEL QUEEN

So she understood that while it may look like I need help, and maybe even I truly do, that doesn't mean I want it. Sometimes I'm just mad about needing help in the first place. And she understood that this whole helping thing can really complicate a friendship.

I never knew this about Jessie and her brother. Who could have guessed, especially the way she acted last year, all weird about my new leg braces. But I figured that was because she didn't even see them like everyone else did, through Sympathy Glasses. She just thought all the attention I was getting was a threat to her popularity, as crazy as that sounds.

The repelling forces of the universe gave me a little gift the next day though. I apparently had a doctor's appointment and didn't have to go to school. Hallelujah!

It wasn't your ordinary doctor's appointment. It was one of those appointments where they do all these tests on you, talk to your parents for hours it seems. It was a whole day thing, in the Big City— Providence! So right after we dropped Chris off at school, me and Mom and Dad hit the open road.

The doctor (Mom said he was a neurologist) did all sorts of wacky things. He poked me here and there, asking, "Ya feel that?" He rubbed this thing on the bottom of my feet, and I guess it was supposed to tickle, but I didn't feel a thing. He moved and stretched my fingers and did all sorts of tests on my hands too. It took forever. Finally, around one o'clock, we headed for home. I was kind of wiped out. While I thought this day off would be a great relief, going through all these tests and stuff made me feel kind of mopey.

I stared silently out the window of the van as Dad pulled onto a city street and headed for the highway to get us home. And straight ahead I saw him—Independent Man.

You've never heard of Independent Man? Well, he's this dude who stands on top of the capitol building in Providence, Rhode Island, which is where the state government meets and does . . . well, I'm not really sure what they do, maybe governmental things? Anyway, Independent Man is really tall, really gold, and has a big spear in his hand. He also has an anchor next to him, which Dad said is a state symbol, seeing as how we're the Ocean State. Dad also told me that for a while, Mr. Independent Man was placed in the Warwick Mall. Like one day you're standing proudly on top of a state building, halfway up to the clouds, and next thing you're hanging out next to the Gap. But then again, Dad said this all happened was when he was a little kid, so maybe Independent Man was standing near the horse and buggy shop instead.

Independent Man got me thinking, though. Will I ever be independent? I looked up at my mom in the front seat, her permanently folded hand on my dad's shoulder. Even though I couldn't hear her, I could tell she was telling him some kind of funny story. She kept flipping her hand back toward herself, then whipping it toward Dad, lightly punching him in the arm. She followed each flip-flop with a big laugh. Her smile was so pretty, but not all blinding like Mr. Goldberg's smile. His was fenced in by his dark mustache and beard, but Mom's smile lit up her whole face. It made me feel warm inside. As Mom babbled on, Dad would nod, slapping the steering wheel and laughing out loud in agreement with this clearly fascinating story. Part of me wanted to hear what she was saying, and part of me just wanted to watch her.

"Dad, what's independence mean?"

Dad called over his shoulder, "It means doing stuff for yourself."

Huh. Mom can't do much for herself. But then again, she's a mom, she's a speech therapist, and she's everything. She used to tell me that she became a speech therapist because she knew she'd have to use her voice to do what her body couldn't. She couldn't pick me up when I was little, or tie my shoes, or help me with my hair. But boy, it's true. She does a lot of talking.

Mr. Independent Man, with your golden skin, your spear and anchor—I've got some questions for you. First of all, why are you lugging around a big weapon and heavy marine equipment? And anyway, what do you know about independence? Is it really all about how shiny and strong and muscular you are? No, I knew I was going to have to figure out my own way to be independent, to do things for myself. And maybe that meant goodbye, Lauren.

Then came the tears again. Darn it! I shook my head hard, making my ponytails fly out to the side like jet planes, just to get that vision of me on the floor of the art room out of my brain. Jessie's words were still ringing in my ears: "Let her float on." I looked out the window and watched the highway lines swoosh by. Then I spotted the gigantic blue termite statue that sits on the roof of a building. Any Rhode Islander can tell you about this big blue

ARLENE, THE REBEL QUEEN

bug, on Route 95 in Providence. And normally, this would be a very entertaining sight for me. But even the bug, even with reindeer antlers on his head for the upcoming holidays, even that didn't make me crack a grin.

Mom had finished her story and turned her smiling face toward me. She took one look at me and the worry wrinkle appeared on her forehead. "What's wrong, Arlene? You're looking so sad."

"Nothin'."

"Hmm. Doesn't look like nothing. Well, what do you think of hot dogs for lunch? We can stop at the New York System diner in Warwick on the way home. How about that?"

I forced my mouth into a smile. "Cool." Mom's attitude toward me had clearly gotten better. Maybe it was because time had passed. Maybe it was watching me go through all those stupid tests today. I didn't really care, even if it was sympathy, as long as I had my mom back. Especially now.

A few minutes later I leaned on a smooth, orange tabletop at the diner with Mom and Dad. This was the only table Mom could get to without a major furniture move. "Nothing like a gag-gah to make my day!"[2] Dad sang and chomped off a big bite of

---

2   Gaggers, usually pronounced gag-gahs, are a Rhode Island specialty!

the little hot dog, covered in chopped onions, meat sauce, and mustard.

"Nothing like a gaggER to kill you, with your cholesterol!" Mom said. She scooped up pieces of salad onto a spoon woven through her fingers.

"Something this yummy can't possibly be bad for you," I said.

"Hey! I haven't seen youz in a while!" A big man in a stained white apron held his hairy arms up in the air and waddled our way. Dad told me he's known Mr. Farrallo since he was a little kid, when he would come here several times a week for gaggers. Must be why his cholesterol is so high now, whatever cholesterol is.

"How are you, Mr. Farrallo?" called Dad. He stood up to give him a hard handshake and slap on the back. "How's business?"

This big diner man's arms plopped down against his middle like a chopped tree hitting the forest floor. "Eh, ya know, up and down, heah and theah, can't complain, can't complain." He leaned toward me, "How ah you, sweetie? Youz doin' good, huh?"

"Um, yeah, sure," I said. "I'm good."

"Aww, that's lovely, deah, that's lovely." He turned back to Dad. "Ah, bizness is okay, but I gotta get all this new equipment. Latest is a new dishwashah.

This one runs, but it's old and needs a paht, so the wife says I gotta just buy a whole new one. Easy for huh to say, eh? They always got somethin' to say, don't they, these wives of ah's?" And he smiled right at mom.

I watched her carefully. "All part of the plan, Mr. Farrallo, all part of the plan to one day rule the world. You better look out!" And then she punched him in the arm. (That must be her laugh signal.)

Ha! Mom is too funny.

But what Mom said gave me a great idea for our protest theater play!

WHEELCHAIR JUMPING

Luckily, everyone has a very short attention span and don't remember things on Monday that happened the Thursday before. So I was in the clear about the art room horror, at least for the time being. Which was good because I had some more serious work to do on my Operation Protest Theater plan.

Step Three. I stood by Mr. Goldberg's desk and waited for him to notice me. No sense in being pushy—yet.

"What can I do for you, Arlene? Did you finish your reading log?"

"Um, yeah, just about. But I wanted to ask you about a project that maybe we could have a little time to work on during social studies class."

Mr. Goldberg narrowed his eyes suspiciously. "What kind of project?"

I gave him a "Who me?" look back. "Oh, it's part of the Recycling Team's action plan. You know, our team with Mrs. Sweeney? Like you said, our sidewalk protest wasn't a good idea. And the Garbage Dump!" I slapped my palm on my forehead. "We really messed up with that one! So Mrs. Sweeney is helping us do like a little information thing after school on Friday, and we have to write out what we're going to say, you know, get it all ready and stuff."

"An information 'thing'?" Mr. Goldberg's left eyebrow arched way up.

I tried to raise one eyebrow too, but on me they both felt connected. How did he do that? I made a mental note to practice that later in front of the mirror.

I went on. "Yeah, like a mini-class or something. You know, where we talk about the importance of recycling and all that. It seemed better than just some posters, but not as messy as dumping garbage. Mrs. Sweeney thought we should do it outside, in the fresh air of Mother Earth, on the playground, so we don't disturb dismissal."

Mr. Goldberg pushed out his lower lip and nodded. "Hmm. Not a bad idea."

I had him. I went in for the slam dunk. "So all the kids on the Recycling Team are finished with their presentations—Jessie and I go today. Maybe we can work on it during social studies this week, or any other free time we have? You know, practice our research, writing, and speaking skills, and all that?" Suh-wish. All net.

"Sure, Arlene, and I'm happy to hear that you and your friends are going to be more productive agents of change this time around. You must have learned something here in class."

"Sure did, Mr. Goldberg, sure did."

Just one more step and everything would be in place. Mwah-ha-ha!

But first, after lunch, it was time for Jessie and me to do our presentation thing. And my thing is poetry.

I smiled at the class, and then went right into it. By the end, they were all clapping out a beat for me!

"Let me tell you 'bout a girl named Jennifer Keelan.
You know she can't walk, she got around by wheelin'.
She made the prez and politicians feel a funny feelin',
When they watched her climb a hundred steps, all
while kneelin'.

At the top she gave a paper to some pol-i-ticians,
Saying we got rights in spite of a disease or condition.
Her picture made the papers, but in the late edition,
And she forced the president to make a quick decision.

Before the ADA was passed, it was A-okay,
To tell folks like us that we should just be locked away.
But now malls, halls, clubs, buses, and cafes,
Have to open up the doors that once blocked our way."

Then, for the last part, with my great Uncle James in mind, I got *dramatic*! I held my two hands up to the sky.

"The words 'We the People' aren't a mystery,
We have rights, freedom and of course, liberty.
When they made civil rights include disability,
The ADA marked its rightful place in history."

I folded my arms in my best Byron-the-militant impression. Everyone was pretty quiet.

"I'm done," I pointed out.

"Oh!" Mr. Goldberg said. "Sorry, Arlene. That was a . . . unique way of presenting the material. Um, does anyone have any questions?"

Joey huffed and raised his hand. "Yeah, I do. What are you talking about?"

I blinked. "The Americans with Disabilities Act,

Joey." I wanted to add "Duh" but I figured Mr. Goldberg would say that was rude.

"But who's this Jennifer chick?" he asked. And then he immediately dove out of his chair because Sheila had reached across the aisle and was about to choke-hold his big, empty, anti-girl-power head.

Mr. Goldberg rushed to stand between them. "Sheila," he warned. "Calm down and get back in your seat. And Joey? Really. That word is disrespectful. You know better."

I needed everyone to pay attention to me again. This was important stuff. "Okay," I clapped my hands. "So picture this! The ADA was written, but then Congress didn't take any action on it. They just let it sit there. And the ADA was going to be huge, because almost every place had to make sure people with disabilities could get in or use their stuff or whatever.

"So a few hundred people planned this protest in Washington, D.C. They went to the building where Congress meets, and they were going to hand politicians a paper with part of the Declaration of Independence written on it. But of course, the Capitol has steps going up to it! And most of the people protesting were using wheelchairs. So they jumped."

"Jumped?" Byron asked, and his mouth opened dentist-wide.

"Yup. Threw themselves out of their wheelchairs and crawled up to the top. Even this eight-year-old girl named Jennifer Keelan. When I read about this . . . well, I just had to express myself. You know? The idea of that, it's just so powerful."

"I understand," Mr. Golberg nodded. "That was an incredible story. I remember seeing that picture in the newspaper. And that kind of intense demonstration really did change things, didn't it?"

"Yeah," I said. "Now with the ADA, you can't be fired because of your disability. Or if you need help to do your job, like my mom, you can get it. Stores need to make sure everything is accessible; information has to be in Braille for people who can't see, and it just goes on and on. It really was a huge change."

"Well, thank you, Arlene for an interesting and informative presentation," Mr. Goldberg said. "Jessie? What do you have for us?"

"Hmph," Jessie began, as she pulled her hair tightly into a ponytail. "What I have for you is even more powerful," and she stared right at me. I wondered when this had become some kind of contest, but whatever. Let her try to top my wheelchair-jumping story.

"*My* law was passed, and like the ADA, it was just sitting there. For *four* years! But then a bunch of people decided to do something about it. And—"

Joey huffed again and raised his hand. "Same question—what are you talking about?!"

Mr. Goldberg more politely said, "Jessie, tell us what law you're focusing on."

Jessie shot a hard look at Joey. "I'm talking about Section 504 of—" she looked down at her report. "Section 504 of the Rehabilitation Act of 1973. It was just a tiny section of a law that wasn't really about rights for people with disabilities. But it was what really started it all. There would be no ADA, no special education laws, no nothing without this first one."

Joey raised his hand again. "Let's get to the part where people jump outta wheelchairs."

Jessie stamped her foot on the floor and glared at Joey. "Are you going to let me do my presentation or not?" She waited, to see if he dared to answer. He knew to be quiet at this point.

"Thank you," she said, without meaning it at all. "Anyway, that's not what happened here. Section 504 is like the ADA. It says you can't discriminate against people just because they have a disability. But it was just sitting there, not doing anything, because no one had written the 'rules' that make it count. And by 1977, four years after the law was passed, people got tired of waiting. So in San Francisco, a bunch of people with disabilities basically took over the offices of the government guys who were supposed to write these rules."

"You mean, like, broke in? Isn't that against the law?" Byron asked.

"Well, I don't know if they busted through doors," Jessie answered, "but yeah, basically they were breaking the law." She shot a look at Joey. "Told you it was better than just jumping out of wheelchairs. And I'm not even done. So these people—again everyone's got a disability—they're like, camping out in these offices. So the government says, 'oh yeah?' and they cut off the phone lines in the offices and blocked any food from getting delivered."

"They couldn't even order pizza?" Sheila cried. "How long could they last?"

Jessie nodded. "You would think not long. But they lasted—" Jessie paused and then leaned toward the class, "twenty-five days."

The class gasped.

"I know," Jessie said. "So here's what happened. Some people snuck food in. One guy smuggled in walkie-talkies for them to talk to people on the outside. Then the mayor of San Francisco helped out. He brought in mattresses and hoses so people could sleep and clean up. I mean, you had people up there in wheelchairs, people who couldn't move, couldn't talk, couldn't breathe without a machine, whatever, and they just camped out for almost a month."

Byron spoke for the whole class when he said, "Wow!"

"Why didn't someone just arrest them though?" Joey wanted to know.

Mr. Goldberg stepped in. "You're right, Joey," he said. "They were breaking the law. But we've seen this before, haven't we? In Byron's report, in Sheila's, and even Joey when you talked about workers who went on strike. It's called civil disobedience. It means you refuse to obey certain laws in order to demonstrate the need for a big change."

"It's risky," Lauren said quietly.

"Yes," Mr. Goldberg agreed. "Yes, it is. I think you kids have found that out, haven't you?"

Jessie, Joey, Sheila, and the gang all looked down, thinking about the painful punishment we were still under from our Garbage Dump.

"But Mr. Goldberg," Jessie said, "from what I was reading, the government just wasn't going to do anything with this law. It would have just sat there—forever, probably. And when the people first took over those offices, it seemed like everyone thought they would just give up if things got hard. It was like a showdown, and the people won!"

"Woo-hoo!" shouted Sheila. She loved a good showdown.

"But wait!" Jessie said. "Here's another interesting thing I found out too. Right after this San Francisco protest, right after Section 504 got going, the government also wrote the rules for another huge law, the one that gives every kid the right to go to public school, even if you have a disability. That had been sitting around for years too. It just seems to me that this protest was huge and like, really worth it."

"Well," Mr. Goldberg said, "I guess that's easy for us to say. We weren't in those offices for twenty-five days. That is the question, isn't it? What's the *right* way to create change?"

"I read about this in my research," Carlos said. "The question people always ask is: do the ends justify the means?"

"Exactly," Mr. Goldberg said.

"Are we supposed to answer that?" Byron wondered out loud.

Mr. Goldberg shook his head. "Don't think you

can. It's one of those questions that you should think about, that in fact, great philosophers have thought long and hard about, but one that may not have an easy answer."

And that was what Mr. Goldberg left us with that day. A question with no right answer. How annoying.

SALES DUD

After school on Tuesday we had to go to the mall, the last place on the planet I wanted to be. Chris needed new sneakers, and Mom and I can't stay home alone for too long, so off we all went. Mom thought we could look for a Christmas outfit for me, but I wasn't in the mood. I had theater on my mind.

We walked around and around. Gosh that boy is picky about his sneakers. I was getting tired from all the walking. I felt like Magellan and the great explorers, suffering great hardships trying to navigate this vast mall area in leg braces.

Mom thankfully suggested that she and I just stay put in the department store near where our car was parked while Dad and Chris checked out a few more stores. I sat down on a chair in the shoe department to rest my weary feet. But a pair of the most awesome boots ever made caught my eye. They were the centerpiece of this kind of sunken display, a small table that was down two steps in the middle of the area, like the star on a stage surrounded by an audience of shoes (everything looked like a theater to me these days!).

I held on to the railing and walked down the two steps to look at the boots more closely. "Ooh, Mom, check these out!" I held the boots up for her to see. She circled her chair around near the edge of the steps, craning her neck to look down at me and the awesome boots.

"I can't see them, Arlene. Bring them up here."

Just then a salesman came over to me. "Can I help you, young lady?"

"Yeah, can I try these on? In a size five?"

"Sure," he said. "Have a seat."

Mom was still trying to maneuver her way closer to me, but there were too many shoe stands, and of course, those two steps. "Arlene," she called through the shoe forest. "What are you doing?"

"I'm just gonna try these on, Mom. See if they fit over my braces."

"No, Arlene, you need to have Dad help. This

man isn't going to know how to fit them over your braces, or whether they'll work for you."

"Oh, I can fit them on her," the salesman said as he came out of the back room carrying boxes of boots.

Mom zipped back and forth now around the edge of the sunken stage. "Arlene, come up here," she called. "Don't take your shoes off! Look, sir, I'm sure you're very good at what you do, but my daughter needs special help to get her shoes on. We need her father here to see if they fit right. And once she gets her shoes off, it's difficult to get them back on without help."

"Oh, I've seen kids in braces before. It's no big deal. These boots should stretch right over them. Here, honey, let's see how they fit."

I was so excited about these cool boots. I ran my hand along the smooth, brown leather.

"Arlene!" Mom was really racing around now, like an angry bee getting ready to sting. "Don't take your shoes off! Come up here, now! And sir, with all due respect, my daughter just isn't a 'kid with braces.' She has Charcot-Marie-Tooth. Are you familiar with that?"

The guy called over his shoulder as he pulled my sneaker off. "Shark tooth—what?"

"Yeah, I didn't think so," Mom snapped as she zoomed around the rim. "Just put the boots away. Thank you for your time. Arlene! Get up here!"

"Wait," I said. "He's almost got them—ouch!"

Mom's wheels buzzed at lightning speed around the circle. "Now!" she yelled.

She was right. She was always right.

I kicked off the boot that the salesman had only half-shoved on my foot and hobbled up to Mom with my one sneaker, one sock situation. The guy followed me. "I'm sure we can find a size that fits you," he called.

"Mom," I pleaded. "Can I please try another size? They're so awesome!"

She shook her head hard. I knew it was risky, but I added one more. "Please?" with a nice high, squeaky tone at the end.

She huffed out a sigh of frustration. "Only thing we can do," she snapped, "is to take them home, and Dad will see if they fit. If not we'll just return them. But—"

"Ah, no, these can't be returned," the guy pointed out. "They're a special sale. No returns."

Mom turned her head slowly to shoot a fierce

glare at this guy. I took a step back. He really should have too.

"Are you saying that," she paused a second, "even though my daughter has a condition that requires special fitting of her shoes, which you obviously know nothing about, that I can't buy these shoes and try them on at home so I have time to see if they fit properly, and then return them, unworn, if they don't fit? Is this what you're saying?"

Mr. Sales Dude started to sweat. He gulped and stammered, "No, um, well, yeah, no, you just . . . um . . . you just can't return them." He added in a weak voice, "I don't really see why we can't try them on here."

"You don't see?" Mom shouted. "You don't see?! Do you see that she wears leg braces? Do you see that she needs special help? Do you know anything about CMT? Do you know that you shouldn't put half your shoe display at the bottom of two steps? Do you realize that I'll never shop here again?"

She turned to me. "And now you have one shoe off. I can't get it back on. You can't get it back on. And certainly *he* can't get it back on!" I knew Mom. She was about to blow up for real. "I can't stay in this store another minute. Arlene, get on."

Well, gee, I hadn't ridden on her lap since I was

a little kid. But she was right, only Dad can get sneakers on over my braces, and it certainly didn't seem like Mom could wait for him to get back. I sat down on Mom's lap, holding my one sneaker in my arms.

And whoosh! Off we went, our hair tangling together behind us in the wind created by the whizzing wheelchair. We zoomed through the store like two racers against ignorance and injustice. Totally cool.

I pumped my fist in the air and shouted: "AND DO YOU EVEN KNOW ABOUT THE ADA?!"

RUCKUS MAKER

Mom and I were stuck in the torture chamber called a mall for a little longer while we waited for Dad and Chris to finish shopping. We had called them on Mom's cell and explained that we needed an ice cream fix, and we needed it immediately. Dad offered to find us and help, but Mom said no, in this day and age, she should be able to easily buy her daughter an ice cream even without the use of her legs or fingers.

But she was wrong.

Mom stretched her neck to see over the counter of the ice cream place in the food court. She tried to order. The teenager who worked there snapped her gum, looked at Mom through half-closed eyes and waited, like she expected Mom to stand up or something. She kept saying, "Whaaat?" because Mom's voice isn't the loudest. CMT affects some people's breathing and voice. Mom can yell just fine at me when we're home, but in a loud mall, trying to make herself heard up and over a stupid glass case of ice cream cakes is tricky. And the gum popper wasn't helping one bit.

After three tries, Mom said, "You're going to have to come around to this side," in the same tone that she uses with me when she's giving orders. The girl shuffled over to us and bent down with her hands on her knees, coach-style, like she was about to tell us to "go long."

"What'll it be?" she said instead, and then snap, chew, bubble, pop.

Mom actually laughed at that point. This girl was funny. "I'll have a scoop of mint chocolate chip and she'll have double fudge. In a cup, please."

The girl stood up and went to work on our order while I fumbled with Mom's wallet to get the money out. Between our four hands and my stiff but at least movable fingers, we managed to get the right number of dollar bills out. "Keep the change," Mom told the girl, then she looked at me and we both laughed, knowing that the last thing we wanted to deal with was putting money *back into* her wallet.

I placed one cup of ice cream on Mom's lap between her knees and held my cup with two hands. We turned to face a sea of small round tables, all squished together in the mall food court with chairs scattered about. The only open table with a chair for me was of course in the middle of this maze, although there was one table at the outer edge, surrounded by three kiddie highchairs. Mom sped up and screeched to a halt in front of the highchairs. Then she spun around to the left, smacking her footrest into one highchair, sending it sliding off to the side. She did the same with one on the right. She was basically playing wheelchair soccer with the highchairs! Some guy sitting nearby jumped up, pushed the last one out of the way, moved the table out a bit, and slid a regular chair over. He nervously patted the seat and looked up at me, as if to say, "Please sit down, little girl, so your mother can stop the target practice with the highchairs."

I plopped down in the seat and called out, "Thank you!" cheerfully. He left the area.

Mom and I giggled and dug into our ice cream. "I think it's time for us to start making a ruckus once in a while," Mom said

My eyes popped open at my mom, and I saw a whole new person there. Well, hel-lo, Rebel Queen!

She smiled a quiet smile. "Just once in a while." She pointed at me with the spoon woven between her fingers. "But you follow *my* lead, Miss Ruckus Maker! There's a time and place for everything, and I don't want any repeats of that Garbage Dump."

I pumped my head up and down quickly. "Of course, of course. You're the captain, Mom." I thought about the play coming up next week. That wouldn't count as a ruckus, would it?

"Well, hi there!" someone called. I looked up and there were the last people on Earth that I wanted to see: Lauren and her mother.

"Hi Sue!" Mom said cheerfully. Then both moms paused, waiting for the same cheery greeting to come from us girls. "Hey," we both mumbled.

The moms looked at us a minute, confused by the sudden change in a lifetime pattern. I tried to fake it, just to avoid this extra attention. "You ready for the play, Lauren?"

Lauren's mom answered instead. "Oh, yes, I saw an email from the PTA that you kids are doing a show about the importance of recycling. How wonderful!"

Boing! Out came Lauren's forehead wrinkle. Oh geez, now what? Couldn't she just fake it along with me?

Lauren turned her worry-face up to her mom. "Mom, didn't you see on the email? I told you, too. The play is the day before my ice-skating tournament. I'm going to have to go to practice," she hissed.

What?! Funny, she didn't tell me, only the director of the play.

Lauren's mom took a big breath in through her O-shaped mouth, and then covered it quickly with her hand. "That's right! Oh no!" Lauren's mom turned to us. "Lauren has been practicing so much for this competition. Did she have a big part in the show, Arlene?"

"Yes," I answered immediately. "A huge part." I glared at Lauren. I *knew* it. I knew she would flake out on me, on us, on the mission!

Lauren's mom had the same worry-face. Ah, this is where she gets it from.

So for a long, awkward minute, they worried and I raged. Mom? I wondered. Newly declared leader of the Rebel Queens . . . any ideas?

"I distinctly remember losing friends when I was your age," Mom said to me quietly.

She had let Lauren and her mom off the hook

gently, like a mature adult would. I would have screamed "Deserter!" but then again, I'm ten and Mom's an old lady.

"Really?" This was shocking to me. Mom had plenty of friends, some who seemed to have known her for centuries.

I had spilled everything to Mom, about that awful art-room scene, about Halloween, and about how it felt like Lauren was getting tired of me in general.

"Really," Mom confirmed. "They just kind of stopped hanging out with me." She looked past me but didn't focus on anything. "It was weird. Even their moms told my mom that they were busy, that they couldn't always be the one helping me." She swallowed but she didn't have any ice cream in her mouth. "It was like they talked about it. And *decided*. You know? They decided I was, like . . . a burden."

I stared at my mother. She stared at something apparently located a million miles behind my head. I waited and watched, copycat to the only person in the world who might have a clue about what I was feeling, my only navigator through this sticky mess.

She turned her head slowly and looked at me. My eyes clung to hers the way I hugged my floatie in the pool's deep end, back when I couldn't swim.

"But other people don't get to decide who or what I am," she said to me. "People are going to come and go in your life, Arlene, and you can't control those changes. You've got enough to do managing your own business, never mind trying to control other people."

"But I don't want to lose Lauren," I said quietly. "Why does she have to be such a runaway?"

"You don't know, and you may never know, what's going on in her head right now. Look, you were friends for a long time. You may get close again in the future. But right now, your relationship has changed, and for a lot of different reasons it sounds like. There's no stopping that. It is what it is."

Is what it is? That's her advice? It was my turn to stare at something a million miles past Mom's head. I thought this whole change thing stunk.

TALENT BOY

Even buried by all these changes, I still had a job to do, a play to direct, and a plan to execute. The show must go on. Step four!

The next day at school, I grabbed a couple of the many overdue books that Joey always shoved to the back of his desk, and headed to visit my favorite librarian at the beginning of lunch.

"Hi Mrs. Sweeney," I called. "Just returning some books."

Mrs. Sweeney was busy rearranging her little round tables into some kind of new order. She huffed and dragged one in each hand to form a figure eight. She mumbled softly to herself, "Gotta get these kindergarteners all up together, like herding a bunch o' puppies."

"Mrs. Sweeney," I called again and held up my books with two hands. "I'm returning these."

"You want a medal?" she answered. "Just put them down on the desk. Thanks."

"Mrs. Sweeney," I called for the third time, worried that she was now getting annoyed. "I need to talk to you about something."

She sighed and walked slowly over to me. "What?"

"Um, so you're in charge of the field and playground schedule, right?"

"Yes, along with the conference room, the auditorium, the gym, and any other thankless job that needs doing around here. Yes, that would be me."

"Wow," I said. "They really do dump it all on you, don't they? They should pay you more!"

And there it was, a teeny half-smile creeping onto her face. Bingo!

"Darn right!" Mrs. Sweeny answered a little more brightly. "Why?"

"Well, you know we all got in trouble after doing that terrible thing with the garbage in Mr. Musgrove's office, right?"

Mrs. Sweeney folded her arms across her chest and squinted her eyes at me. "Hmm, yes, I did hear about that. Not the smartest thing in the world, was it?"

"No," I looked down and shook my head. "No, not at all. Very dumb actually. It's like we just lost our brains." And I slapped the side of my supposedly hollow skull.

Mrs. Sweeney nodded. "And what does any of this have to do with me?"

"Okay, yeah, so Mr. Goldberg thinks we took the things we've been learning about in social studies and went totally the wrong way. So he wants to teach us a lesson too. He told us to clean up the blacktop and playground area outside. It's like getting community service for our crime or something. Kind of makes sense, and really, it fits into our recycling team anyway. So Mr. Goldberg told me to ask you to make sure the blacktop area isn't being used this Friday after school, by the aftercare or sports classes or whatever."

"Well," Mrs. Sweeney rubbed her forehead and picked up a clipboard. She flipped over a few papers, kind of violently, until she got to the one she wanted. "Well, we don't have any sports on Fridays. I'll just make sure the aftercare stays inside while you're out there. What do you need, like an hour or so?"

"Yep, that would be perfect," I answered.

"'Kay, done. But make sure you clean it up well.

Don't just wander around dragging a trash bag along behind you, like I've seen other do-gooder groups do."

"Of course!" I said. "We'll do such a good job, you'll be able to eat off the playground!"

We both kind of shuddered at that thought. Why do I always go too far?

We didn't get a chance to work on the play again until Thursday afternoon. What pressure! One day away, so much rehearsing to do, and we had lost one of our main actors!

"Okay, we've got problems," I told the group. "Lauren bailed on us."

Jessie spat out a puff of air, an unspoken "I told you so."

"So we need someone to play her part," Carlos said, stating the obvious. "Arlene, you do it." This was not so obvious.

"But the whole point of me not playing a major part was that I could do all the behind-the-scenes director things!" I said.

"Too bad," Sheila answered. "This isn't Broadway. How much is there to do behind the scenes?"

"But how am I going to play two parts—the one

I was going to play plus Lauren's? They're in a scene together!"

"Good point," Byron admitted. "We need to find someone else to help us."

None of us wanted to involve any outsiders in our scheme. It was too risky. We had built a shaky house of cards around this play, and any newcomer meant possible destruction.

"I'll take care of it. This is my responsibility." I was the director after all. I had to handle this for my people, for the good of the show, for the success of our mission.

I had absolutely no idea what I could do. But I knew I had to manage my business.

That night at home, I was stressing. I managed to get through my homework and dinner, but then I couldn't stop my mind from spinning. I plopped onto the floor in front of the couch, legs stretched out under the coffee table. This was my favorite chill-spot. Something about being low, resting my head on the couch cushion, zoning in front of the TV was all very relaxing.

As I was chilling, trying to allow the forces of the universe to reveal the answer to my actor-shortage problem, Chris came over and flopped his big body down on the couch, resting his calves on my shoulders like I was the coffee table!

"Get OFF!" I screamed.

"Oh sorry, I didn't see you there," Chris smirked.

"Liar!"

Chris reached over and grabbed the remote from the coffee table with his octopus arms, quickly switching to the sports channel.

"Put it BACK!" I screamed again. I was going to get a sore throat from this crazy man, the night before my big play!

"I can't watch one more singing, dancing, talent contest!" Chris moaned, as he slid his long fingers down his face, stretching his cheeks, leaving bloodshot, rolled-up eyeballs to stare at me.

"Ew. You're disgusting," I mumbled and turned away. "You wouldn't know talent if it smacked you in that monster face of yours."

He snorted. "Oh, Chris Harper's got talent!" He hurled himself up from the couch with an energy I can honestly say I had never seen before within the body of my brother, and he began tap dancing in front of me on the coffee table. Well, I mean, kind of shuffling in his socks would be a better description, but I couldn't stop the giggle from coming out of my mouth. I slapped my hand over my face to block it from giving him any satisfaction.

"Uh-huh, that's what I'm talking 'bout. TAL-ENT!" Chris flipped his feet even faster back and forth.

Dad walked in just then, stopped and stared. "What in the world?"

As I watched Chris's feet move, as Dad and I stared at this goofy guy, it hit me. Talent! My play! Lauren, the deserter! CHRIS!

"Hey, Talent Boy!" I shouted. "Have I got a gig for you!"

And I explained it all to my big brother. And my big brother came through for me.

THE SHOW MUST GO ON

The sun burst into the sky that Friday morning. I saw it with my own eyes, because it felt like the middle of the night when I had to get up, thanks to winter stealing my daylight. Dad gets up at 4:30 every day. Any wake-up time that starts with a 4 is like squished bug-guts, just eww. I get to sleep until 6, which is a much more reasonable time for humans to wake up, but still early, still as dark as the back of the hall closet, my favorite manhunt hiding place. (Shh. Don't tell anyone!)

But by the time I was brushing my teeth after breakfast, I saw it, the sun climbing to its top spot above the Earth. I smiled at it. It streaked its light my way, as if to say, "Good luck, girl!" I nodded and said "Thanks!"

"Crazy pills in your cereal again, Sis?" Chris bumped me to the side to grab his toothbrush. "Who you talking to?"

I steadied myself and punched him as hard as I could in the arm. "Shut up! I'm having a moment on like, the biggest day of my life, so you can just . . . shut up!" I know, not my best comeback. All my creative juices were focused on the play.

"You'd better be nice to your star," Chris smiled and pretended to pat his face with make-up in the mirror. "Okay, see you after school. And I want sparkling water, cupcakes, and mints in my dressing room, but only spearmint, no peppermint."

I spit a glob of toothpaste into the sink to answer his request. "Be there or you're dead."

School, of course, was endless. The gang was all pumped up, all except Lauren who looked like a lost puppy dog, or like the owner of a lost puppy, all weepy and wandering.

But I had to float on, as Jessie would say.

The dismissal bell finally rang, and we burst out onto the playground. Just about every kid in the school had heard about our play, and they all ran down toward the blacktop and basketball court, which was kind of at the bottom of a valley. It wasn't like the Grand Canyon, but there was enough of a hill on all sides of the court that after a good rain, we basically had a basketball lake, like we could play water polo or something. If we were lucky enough that it rained and then got cold (standard practice in Rhode Island), we had a fantastic ice rink! But today, for the play, all was good. Dry, sunny, and not even that cold for a winter day. And the hill made it possible for a larger audience to still see the show. Couldn't have planned it better if I'd built it myself!

I got busy setting up our props: the crystal ball, the map of our universe, our Recycling Team posters "recycled" into picket signs for Scene 3. Byron had made a crazy alien costume and was busy arranging his sonic radar hat. I looked up from the million things I had to do and saw a crowd swelling like my forehead that time Chris whacked me by accident with his Wiffle bat.

Chris! Where was Chris?!

I searched the crowd for my brother, for my only hope that the show could go on without Lauren. But what I saw made me suck in a breath.

It wasn't Chris. It was Mrs. Landers, the PTA lady, talking with Mr. Goldberg!

No, no, no! These people cannot talk to each other!

They were off in the distance, a few yards behind the last of the growing audience. But I could see them enough to understand what they were saying, and it was not good.

I saw Mrs. Landers rest her hand gently on Mr. Goldberg's shoulder. She nodded and smiled and gabbed. Mr. Goldberg looked confused. He shook his head. Mrs. Landers shook her head and tilted it to the side, as if to say, "Really? You didn't ask me to tell all the parents about a school play put on by your social studies class?"

Then they both shook their heads and looked toward me.

Yikes!

"Welcome!" I screamed with every ounce of strength my vocal cords could muster. I screamed the rest all in one word to save time: "Thank-you-for-coming-let's-get-this-show-started-scene-one!" Kids, parents, and whoever else had wandered onto the playground got quiet and turned toward the "stage." Jessie, Byron and I took our places and began.[3]

---

3   The entire play is included at the back of the book.

"A half century ago," Byron said, "on a far-away planet called Loodle Doodle. . ."

The play started out great. Jessie was born to play an alien leader (not surprising). "We must take over Planet Earth," she shouted. "It is the key to our taking over the entire universe!" She flung both of her arms into the air, like the universe really did belong to her. And Byron stole the show with his awesome alien costume. But for me, it was like my ghost said my lines. I had no memory of scene 1 at all. I kept searching for Chris and watching the drama unfold back behind the crowd.

Between scene 1 and scene 2, Mrs. Sweeney joined Mr. Goldberg and Mrs. Landers. OMG! Don't these teachers have papers to correct, or work to do, or something?!

Scene 2 began with all of us staring at our home-made crystal ball. My heart thumped inside my chest as I kept looking around for Chris. I saw Mrs. Sweeney behind the audience, waving her hands in the air, pointing toward the court, and then waving some more, as if to say, "Didn't you ask me to clear the playground so the kids could clean it up? Looks like a lot of drama, not much cleaning!" Mr. Goldberg shrugged and shook his head, then held his hand, palm up, toward Mrs. Sweeney, probably saying, "No, my dear, *you* asked me to let the kids plan an information session out here today." Then Mrs. Sweeney stood up on her tiptoes and socked Mr. Goldberg in the arm, followed by more finger wagging at his nose.

Were we going to need someone to break up a fight out there?

I was so focused on those teachers that I was caught off guard for my line. "Um . . . But what about the weekends?" I said. "Oh no! I mean, *weakness*. What about the weakness?" Jessie glared at me for messing up.

She made up for my mistake with a terrific performance, though, doing this great evil laugh when she announced that the universe would be "mine, all mine!" We managed to get through scene 2 but there was still no sign of Chris, and a teacher brawl was about to break out behind the audience. My short career as theater director was about to slam into a brick wall!

As we were getting ready for scene 3, I heard a low voice from behind my back. "How are you youngsters of Greenwood School doing on this fine day?" Was that Mr. Musgrove?

No, it was Chris! Wow, what an amazing actor!

He even fooled his own sis! He was wearing his best suit jacket, dress shoes, a tie, and even a bald cap!

"Get out there on stage you awesome brother! You saved my life! For now," I added with a sense of dread as I looked over at the three adults about to discover my web of lies.

Scene 3 began with Sheila, Joey, and Carlos as "students" chanting, "One bottle, one tray, that's all it takes to save the day! One tray, one can, to save the Earth, that's our plan!" The audience was really getting into it, and they started chanting along with the actors. They loved Chris as Mr. Fusgrove. That got a huge laugh. And during the final standoff between the aliens and the students, when Carlos's character invited the audience to come up and join the students, they filled the stage!

Then it was my turn to deliver the final lines of the play. I stepped forward but sucked in a breath when I saw that Mr. Musgrove had joined Mr. Goldberg and the others. I could almost hear him, "I thought these kids were cleaning up the playground! Mrs. Landers, just what is going on here?" Mrs. Landers put her hand over her heart, as if to say, "I know nothing! I'm innocent." Mrs. Sweeney wasn't buying any of it, and her head was shaking back and forth like my Patriots bobblehead statue.

I was shaking as I stepped forward and stumbled over my lines: "As the famous Margaret Mead once said, 'A s-small g-g-group of thoughtful people, um, could change the world. Indeed . . .'" I took a deep breath to gain control. Even if it was the final line of my theatrical career, I would make it count! "'Indeed, it's the only thing that ever has.'"

The audience jumped to its feet, clapping and cheering. Boy, they were into it all right, but as I saw all four of my soon-to-be-accusers marching toward the stage, I knew I had to be *out* of it. Carlos raised his hand and shouted to the audience, "Join us! Use the power of one! Become a powerful force to save our planet!" Kids, parents, neighbors, even stray dogs began to gather around the Pied Piper Carlos, with everyone talking at once about ways to make Greenwood School more green. I would have loved to stick around and watch the great results from all our hard work, but I was on the run!

I worked my way up the hill, toward the safety of my parents. Surely Mom would have my back. Just as I huffed my way to the top, a hand reached out from above to help pull me to flat land. Jessie! Not again! Enough rescuing by my archenemy. But it made sense once again to use her help, and I held on with two hands as she yanked me up.

"Arlene!" she said. "We did it! Look at all of them! Things are really going to change around here!"

"Yep, you bet! Good show! Anyway, bye! Gotta go home," and I tried to make my escape.

"Nice math lesson," a boy's voice said.

I turned back again and saw some tall guy standing next to Jessie. "Hey, Arlene, this is my brother Robert," Jessie said as she jerked a thumb in his direction. "He liked the play."

"I didn't say that," Robert corrected, staring at the ground next to my feet. Was he looking at my leg braces? Whatsa matter? Never seen leg braces before, buddy?

"What?" I asked. "You didn't like it?" With this guy being a big stare-monster and an even bigger critic, I forgot about my escape for a second, folded my arms and scowled at him. Bring it, Robert.

"I didn't say that either," Robert replied, moving his stare up to my left earlobe. "I didn't say anything about liking it or not liking it. I said, if you were *listening*, that it was a good math lesson."

"It wasn't a math lesson!" I said.

"What do you mean, math lesson?" Jessie asked her big brother, and shot me a glare like, *Relax!*

Let's find out what he's talking about before you get all offended.

"Exponents," Robert said.

I waited. Jessie waited. But apparently, the one word was the explanation.

Okay, now I was curious. "Robert, whaddya mean exponents? The play was about recycling and saving the Earth by wasting less, being more green."

Robert stared at the sky, smirking. "Green had nothing to do with that play. It was a math lesson about exponents, how you take one, then expand by one, then those two each expand by one, and then those four expand by one. Pretty soon, you're into the millions. It's simple exponents. Cool math lesson."

I stared right at this guy. Exponents? What in the world?

Then I remembered what Jessie told me about Robert, how he saw things differently sometimes because he has autism. She was right! Who would have thought my play was about math? Not even me, the girl who wrote it! "Cool" is right on!

"Thanks, Robert! Glad you liked it—"

"I didn't say I liked it!"

"Oh, right, sorry. Umm, did you find it funny though?"

"Funny? No. And a lot of it made no sense. Yoda would never fly with those kids. You made him look like an idiot, and he was really one of the best Jedi Masters."

"Yeah, Arlene," Jessie interjected, "next time we should have Robert read it over before we perform it in front of a live audience. He'll be able to correct all of your mistakes."

"Huh. Yeah, sure." I did like talking to this Robert guy, but Mr. Musgrove and his gang were gaining ground. "Thanks, but gotta go!" I said and hurried toward Mom and Dad. They wanted to hang around and gush over my theatrical success, but I rushed them out of there.

FLOATING ON

One, two, three, four. Four pairs of folded arms. And let's see, one, two, three, four. Four sets of tapping toes.

I could make a children's picture book out of this scene: One, two, three, four. Four adults about to roar. Four, three, two, one. Arlene's fun is just about done!

Mr. Musgrove spoke first. I was sitting in a chair in his office, first thing Monday morning, and these four adults were lined up in in front of me to discuss the ruckus I had caused on Friday. I had tucked my hands under my thighs and was staring at the floor, trying to look pitiful and sorry.

But I was not sorry for my play. I would never be sorry for saving Mother Earth! (I was, however, very sorry for lying to these guys.) Still, what choice did I have? Sit around and do nothing? What would Uncle James have thought of me?

"Arlene," Mr. Musgrove began. "What you did was completely unacceptable. You lied to your teacher, your principal, the PTA, and I can't imagine—"

"And to her librarian!" Mrs. Sweeney barked, turning her folded arms to Mr. Musgrove.

Mr. Musgrove shot an annoyed glance at Mrs. Sweeney for interrupting his flow. "You lied to all of us and manipulated people so you could get what you wanted. You were dishonest, and I won't have this in my school. Do you understand me, young lady?"

I knew. I knew in my head that I should nod, continue to stare at the floor, keep my hands under my thighs, even sigh, all sad-like. Oh, I knew the part I should play in this drama, knew it only too well.

But my heart—no, make that my gut—screamed something else. This was not how the story should end. This was not about me being sneaky and manipulative and a liar. This was about me believing in something and trying to make things change in my school, for a good purpose! Doesn't that count?

Do the ends justify the means? I remembered Mr. Goldberg's question to us. He said there was no clear answer. Well, to me, in that moment, I really thought the ends did justify the means. We didn't dump garbage, didn't ruin anybody's office this time. We told our ideas to the people, in a fun, even polite, way. So there were a few fibs in the beginning—did they erase all the other good stuff?

I took my hands out from under my legs. I looked up. Then I stood up. I spoke in my strongest voice, and I stared right at these four people.

"We have to do more," I said. "We waste and throw out so much garbage in this school, and there are so many ways we can be more responsible citizens of this planet. Our Recycle Team wasn't going to do anything but put up some posters. That does nothing except use up more cardboard that we're not even going to recycle!"

Mr. Goldberg stepped forward and pulled up a chair beside me, sitting his tall body down so he could look at me eye level. "Arlene, we know you believe strongly in your ideals, your 'mission' if you want to call it that. But just like we talked about in class, there are right ways to go about making changes. Lying to your teachers was not the right way."

"But if I had asked to put on a play, what would the answer have been?"

"Would have been a heck-no!" Mrs. Sweeney shouted. "How many activities am I going to have to run around here?"

"Arlene," Mr. Musgrove took over. "You barely finished serving your consequences from the last inappropriate thing you did in the name of your mission," saying that last word like it hurt his teeth to pronounce it. "So, no, you wouldn't have been given permission to stage some kind of rally on the playground. You need to understand that you're one little girl and you don't run the show."

"I do understand that, Mr. Musgrove. I understand it perfectly. Yes, I am one person . . . but actually, I can change the world."

And then I busted through that row of adults like a fierce Patriot linebacker.

I stopped for a second at the door. "Just let me know what my punishment is for this one, and I'll serve it." And out of that office I went, steadier than I had ever been in the new braces.

I turned left to go back to my classroom, feeling like I was flying down the hallway. And there she was, coming toward me.

There was no bubbling of icky feelings in my stomach this time when I saw Lauren. I mean, the play was over, it was a huge success, and I did it without the help of my "help-ah." I was feeling . . . yes, independent.

"Hey Lauren," I said, casually.

She looked up at my face and smiled. "Hey!"

Then, nothing. Neither of us said anything for like, a whole minute.

I jumped in. "How'd the skating tournament go?"

She sighed. "Eh, I placed in the middle. I've got more practicing to do, for sure."

"Well, it was your first one, right? You'll get there."

She smiled again, all warm. "Thanks."

Another long minute of silence. A bird chirped outside the hallway window.

"I heard the play was really cool."

"Yeah, it was!"

"I'm sorry I missed it."

I smiled all warm this time. "Me too. You would've had fun. I think things are really going to change now."

Just then, Maddie passed by us on her way to the bathroom. "Hey, Lauren, see you at practice Saturday!"

Lauren called back, "Yep! See you then." She looked back at me and sighed. "Yeah, I think things are really going to change now too."

During the next long pause in our conversation, I swear I heard time itself passing by.

I took a big breath and ended it. "Hey, so see you later! Good luck on the next tournament!"

She looked right at me with those big, cocoa eyes. "Thanks, Arlene. See you later."

"So when are you moving to Rhode Island, Uncle James?" I asked excitedly. We were cruising around near the beaches in his sporty black car, just me and my Unc, spending some quality time together during my winter break. Uncle James and Aunt Marie had come to Rhode Island to "house hunt."

"Soon as we find a place to crash, Whopper Stopper."

"Cool. Can't wait to be more of a full-time cousin!"

"Me too. Little Zoe's going to need a good role model. You know, besides me." Uncle James stared at the road a minute. "Oh, yeah, and her mom." He smiled at me. "Who else is going to show her how to create a ruckus?"

I laughed. "Yeah, well, my ruckus making is taking a break right now. I'm enjoying my latest victory for a little while."

I smiled as I thought about that victory. After I had made my grand exit from Mr. Musgrove's office, those grown-ups must have got to talking. Mr. Musgrove roped me aside with a hooked finger as I was walking to the bus after school later that day. We sat together on the long bench in the main hallway, two folks negotiating a deal that would be a win-win.

I was a pro at this, like when I worked out a peace treaty between the boys and girls last year. Mr. Musgrove needed to show he was doing something to save the Earth because the full force of the play's audience was on his back—parents, neighbors, even teachers joined in to argue that Greenwood needed to be more green. They wanted action, not just posters. But there was no money in the budget for anything major.

That's when I had an idea. I'm tempted to say a "brilliant idea," but I don't want all this to go to my head. I told my principal about my buddy Mr. Farallo, the guy at the hot dog joint in Warwick. He needed to find a new home for his old dishwasher, which, with the addition of just a teeny part, would work well enough to handle some trays and forks in our cafeteria. Mr. Musgrove loved this. He'd get a lot of credit for not much money—a principal's dream. It would be a beautiful victory for me too! And of course, I agreed to serve out an additional punishment, no recess until April vacation! But that was fine with me. The lying really was wrong.

Uncle James had been so proud of me and my victory! But now, staring out at the beaches as we drove, Uncle James seemed preoccupied.

"Let's walk on the beach, 'Lene-y," he said.

"Dude, it's thirty degrees outside."

"Just for a minute. I gotta breathe some fresh ocean air."

We stood on Scarborough Beach's wooden ramp, something I always remembered being there but Mom often told me of the old days when she was shut out of the beach's smooth, wheelchair-trapping sand by a whole bunch of steps.

"C'mon Arlene, I'll help you. Let's walk on the beach, just feel the sand between our toes, see how cold the water is."

I went along with my crazy Uncle, loving the fact that if Mom knew we were doing this, she'd be screaming. He helped me get my sneakers, braces and socks off. Unlike the sales guy at the mall, Uncle James knew how to do this. Then he propped me up with his strong arms as we hobbled toward the water. Luckily it was high tide, and we got to wet sand fairly quickly.

Ah! Even with CMT, I could feel the water was frigid! "My toes are going to fall off, Uncle James!"

"Just a few steps. Let's leave our footprints."

Uncle James turned to face me, holding both my hands and stepping carefully backwards as I made my way forward. We smiled into each other's faces.

"You okay with moving here to Rhode Island?" I asked.

Uncle James sighed out a heavy breath. "Okay? Yeah, I'm okay. Things are changing at lightning speed. What can I do, step off? Quit? You and I are no quitters."

"Got that right."

"No, it's going to be—"

I tried to finish his sentence. "Going to be all right?"

"Nah, it's just going to be." He stared at the roaring water. "Know what I mean?"

I thought of Lauren. "I do, Uncle James, I do."

He put his arm around me and we walked back to dry, slightly warmer sand. Then Uncle James turned to look behind us. I did the same. Our footprints had tracked a crooked line, like two people trying really hard to make their way through a lot of obstacles. Suddenly that fierce ocean leaped up and smashed down on our footprints, erasing all but the ones right near us.

"And they're gone," Uncle James whispered, to no one really.

I shivered. Uncle James threw his hoodie around my shoulders and said, "Let's go get some ice cream!"

Oh happy day! I thought.

"I think I'm going to like it here, Chilly Nilly," Uncle James said.

"I think so too, Uncle James!"

THE POWER OF ONE

Scene 1

NARRATOR (Byron, offstage): A half century ago, on a far-away planet called . . . Loodle Doodle, the president's council holds a very important meeting.

LOODLE-DOODLE LEADER (Jessie): We must take over planet Earth. It is the key to our taking over the entire universe! Look! *She points to a map of the planets in the universe she plans to take over—four red circles and a big Earth in the shape of a five-point star.* Once we get Earth, we'll have a star! And that would make my map very pretty.

LOODLE DOODLE FIRST LIEUTENANT (Arlene): Who cares what shape it makes? Do we really want to take over the Earth? They're so whiny down there.

LOODLE DOODLE SECOND LIEUTENANT (Byron): I don't know. I think they're kind of cute. Look at that thing they just invented—what do they call it—a tel-ee-vision? I mean they sing, they dance—they're adorable!

LEADER: No! It's not about adorable! And I don't care whether earthlings whine. In order to be the most powerful aliens in the universe—and to make my map look like a pretty star—I must take over the Earth! And I know exactly how to do it! Listen up, my good council, the secret to taking over the Earth is to . . . allow them to destroy the planet themselves! I don't care if it's a big, brown chunk of smoking rock, it still makes me a pretty star.

FIRST LIEUTENANT: Why would earthlings destroy their own planet? That makes no sense!

LEADER: Oh, but they already are, my good friend, they already are. Look at all the factories, the pollution, the waste that is happening there. It is only a matter of time!

SECOND LIEUTENANT: Hmm, but how can we be sure they won't stop all that polluting? I mean, won't they realize what they're doing and change? They're pretty smart. They invented this little box that you can stare at and be entertained by, without talking to anyone, or getting any exercise at all. You just sit there eating potato chips and getting lazy . . . *voice trails off.* Hmm. Maybe not so smart.

LEADER: I have the answer, my friends. And this is why I am the leader and you are the lieutenants. The answer is . . . *pause, pronounce with a long "a"* . . . the power of a one!

FIRST LIEUTENANT: The answer . . . is steak sauce?

LEADER: No! Let me rephrase: the Power of One! *Stretches up both hands above head in triumph.* The power of one will make sure that they destroy their own planet. The only problem is that there is a single weakness in this power. Let me explain.

The three huddle together and whisper as the scene ends.

Scene 2

NARRATOR: Fast-forward *makes fast-forward/zipping noises* to today. The Leader's Council sits together watching the planet Earth on their special crystal ball.

FIRST LIEUTENANT: *Excited.* It's working! It's working! The Power of One!

SECOND LIEUTENANT: Wow! One plastic bottle thrown away here, one Styrofoam tray thrown away there, one trash can full of paper dumped into a landfill instead of recycled, this is all it takes. One here, one there, one everywhere. And soon, everyone's doing it! Everyone is contributing to the destruction of their own planet! And because they do it one at a time, no one thinks that what they're doing makes any difference! Who would have thought this would ever work?

LEADER: *Clears throat.* Me! That's who! It's only a matter of time now.

FIRST LIEUTENANT: But what about the weakness?

LEADER: Well, so far, the weakness hasn't happened. Maybe we'll have a run of good luck, and it never will. And then, the pretty little five-point star will be mine, all mine! *Evil laugh.*

SECOND LIEUTENANT: But wait! What's going on down there? *All three bend closer to their crystal ball.* That's a school. Let me see if I can read it . . . yes, Greenwood School. Something's happening there, Leader! Look!

Scene 3

Greenwood School playground

MEELA, MOEY, AND BARLOS: *Chanting, marching in a circle, like at a protest or rally, carrying signs supporting "green" efforts.* One bottle, one tray, that's all it takes to save the day! One tray, one can, to save the Earth, that is our plan!

MEELA: *Calling out to group.* Come on people! All it takes is *one.* Just each *one* of you, if you do your part, we can make a difference, a big difference!

MR FUSGROVE: *Puts arm around shoulders of Moey and Meela.* You kids are just wonderful. What would Greenwood School do without you? Thank you for leading our community in this campaign to save the planet. How can we show our gratitude?

MOEY: Well, Mr. Fusgrove, how about we switch things around: vacation for nine months, school for three?

MR FUSGROVE: A fabulous idea, son! That way, you can do more to save Mother Earth!

MEELA, MOEY, BARLOS: Hip-hip hooray! *Chanting again.* One bottle, one can, one Styrofoam tray. That's all it takes to save the day!

Mr. Fusgrove smiles proudly. An angry voice is heard from off-stage.

LEADER: Drat, drat, and double-drat!

BARLOS: Did you hear something?

MEELA: *Crosses arms, looks angry.* Did somebody call me fat?

The three aliens from Loodle Doodle move onstage, from stage left. The Greenwood students continue to march in a small circle, not noticing the aliens.

LEADER: The weakness! It happened! The . . . *said in a disgusted voice* KIDS found out!

FIRST LIEUTENANT: The weakness! These darn kids never believe anything they're told. It's like they have minds of their own!

SECOND LIEUTENANT: How dare they think for themselves!

LEADER: The kids are using our own secret Power of One weapon against us. They must be stopped! *Leader races toward the students, with the two Council following behind.* Stop this non-sense! Stop this instant!

The students are startled at first, but then they crowd together to face the aliens in defense.

BARLOS: First of all, who *are* you, and I don't believe we need to stop anything. We have permission to be here and speak our minds.

LEADER: That's the problem! You young people are always *makes dramatic air quotes and in a whiny voice* "speaking your minds." Why don't you just do what you're told? That's what kids do on our planet, and that's why we're about to take over the whole universe, because we have *shouts like a rap singer* order in the house!

SECOND LIEUTENANT: Please forgive our Leader's manners, *reaches out to shake Barlos's hand* I'm second lieutenant, and this is my best bud, first lieutenant. The screaming one is our leader.

MEELA: You're from another planet?! Did you bring Yoda?

SECOND LIEUTENANT: No way, he's too high-maintenance to travel with! He needs a special booster seat in the rocket ship so he can see out the window, and then he keeps zinging objects all around just to show off the Force. Totally annoying.

LEADER: Enough! Puh-lease! Can we get to the point?! We demand that you stop protesting and go back to doing what everybody else was doing, throwing things away and wasting stuff!

MOEY: We will not! We demand that you go back to doing whatever it is you were doing, taking care of Yogi Bear or whoever.

MEELA: *Laughing, leaning toward Moey.* It's Yo-Da!

BARLOS: With all due respect, we'll do what has to be done to stand up for what we believe in. And you can't stop us.

FIRST LIEUTENANT: Oh yeah? What are three little kids going to do against three tough aliens?

BARLOS: Are you forgetting something? We know the Power of One. It just takes one, then one, then one, and then one. And soon you have the strength of a whole army! *Turns toward the audience.* Come stand with us if you believe in the Power of One! *Audience members come and stand with the students. The aliens scream, cry, and melt to the ground when faced with the force of the Power of One, like the Wicked Witch in the* Wizard of Oz *when drenched with water. Once the three are on the floor, defeated, everyone cheers and shouts "Power of One!"*

As Arlene did in the story, one actor/actress or the whole group can announce at the end of the play the quote from Margaret Mead: A small group of thoughtful people could change the world. Indeed, it's the only thing that ever has.

NOTE TO READERS

Charcot-Marie-Tooth (CMT) is a complicated-sounding disease. It affects a lot of people, about 2.6 million around the world.

It is the most common nerve disorder that can be inherited, although as Arlene points out, it's not always passed down from a family member. Sometimes it just shows up without anyone else in the family having it.

There are many different types of CMT, too, and it can affect kids and adults in lots of different ways. The girl who inspired this book series has CMT, and her name is Grace Caldarone (seen here with her mom). Grace and her mom want to let people know about CMT and what it's like to live with it.

But remember, this is fiction, after all. We made up the actual story. No, Grace didn't really dump garbage on her principal's office floor! The ideas in this book, though, are very real. CMT, like a lot of things, can be challenging, so it's important for us to understand it. The more we understand about each other's challenges, the better we can support each other.

Even more importantly, the more we understand CMT, the better chance we have of finding a cure for it! Think of it, all those millions of people could one day get treatment and be able to freely move their arms and legs again. This is something that Grace and her mom dream about a lot, and so they are working really hard to make it happen.

You can help find a cure too! Schools and communities can create a "Team CMT" and raise money for research. See www.hnf.donorpages.com/ TEAMCMTKIDS/ for more details. To learn more about CMT, check out the Hereditary Neuropathy Foundation website at www.hnf-cure.org.

As Arlene learned, each of us has the power to change the world. We really do. Just start with your corner, your neighborhood, your school, and you'll be amazed at what you can accomplish!

ACKNOWLEDGMENTS

Carol and Marybeth would like to thank the many, many people who believed in and supported this book and the Arlene series. We are incredibly grateful to the hundreds of family members and friends who donate their talent, time, and treasure to Grace's Courage Crusade. It is because of you that we will make a difference for Grace and all the children like her growing up with CMT. We also couldn't have done any of this without the incredible support from the Hereditary Neuropathy Foundation and its leader, Allison Moore. Thank you for believing in us and our vision for this book project!

We'd like to also thank those who helped with the writing and production of this book. We appreciate our readers for their valuable time, expertise, and editorial analysis, especially Jennifer Alessi McGinley, Nadya Hosein, and Lenka Vodicka. A special thank you goes out to our most critical readers, Grace Caldarone and Jaden Liu. We are especially grateful to Mark Minnig for the many hours and special talent he contributed for the cover illustration, even when left with no power by Hurricane Sandy! Thanks also to Stan Mack for invaluable guidance on many issues, including the artwork. Finally, we have tremendous appreciation for all of the advice and support from the folks at Greenleaf Book Group.

ABOUT THE AUTHORS

Carol grew up in Rhode Island, enjoying coffee milk and ignoring Rs in words—until she met Marybeth, a New Yorker who was studying to become a speech therapist at the University of Rhode Island. Marybeth first fixed Carol's speech, and then they became best friends. They joined forces to help find a cure for Charcot-Marie-Tooth (CMT) disease, which affects both Marybeth and her daughter, Grace. All proceeds from this book will be donated to the Hereditary Neuropathy Foundation to fund CMT research, develop new treatments, and hopefully find a cure.

Carol Liu is an attorney and clinical social worker working with children who have special needs in the Washington, D.C. area. Other books include the first book in this series, *Arlene On the Scene*, and *True Friends*, a children's picture book.

Marybeth Sidoti Caldarone is a speech/language pathologist helping children in public schools in southern Rhode Island. She is actively involved in the network of organizations committed to finding a cure for CMT.